YORK NOTES

General Editors: Professor A.N. Jeffares (*University of Stirling*) & Professor Suheil Bushrui (*American University of Beirut*)

Joseph Conrad

HEART OF DARKNESS

Notes by Hena Maes-Jelinek

Licence, PH D (LIÈGE)
Chargé de cours, University of Liège, Belgium

**LONGMAN
YORK PRESS**

YORK PRESS
Immeuble Esseily, Place Riad Solh, Beirut.

LONGMAN GROUP UK LIMITED
Longman House, Burnt Mill, Harlow,
Essex CM20 2JE, England
Associated companies, branches and representatives
throughout the world

First published 1982
Eighth impression 1991

ISBN 0-582-02269-X

Produced by Longman Group (FE) Ltd.
Printed in Hong Kong

Contents

Part 1

Introduction

Joseph Conrad's life

Joseph Conrad has a unique position in English letters: he wrote in a language that was not native to him, and his novels have little in common with the comedy of manners that was fashionable when he began to write. His real name was Joseph Teodor Konrad Nalęcz Korzeniowski. He was born on 3 December 1857 in a part of Poland that was under Russian domination. His parents were ardent patriots who belonged to the Polish landed gentry and bitterly resented the partition of their country between Russia, Germany and Austria. His father, who had a chivalrous and romantic temperament, injudiciously took part in a revolution that failed. He was arrested and exiled to the north of Moscow. His wife insisted on sharing his exile, with their little boy; she died of the hardship they endured when Conrad was seven. His father's health also failed and he died after their return to Poland, when Conrad was eleven. Conrad seems to have remembered from his father's personality the qualities of duty, courage and fidelity which he so much admired and which are later to be found in some of the characters in his novels.

After his parents' death Conrad was placed under the care of his maternal uncle, Thaddeus Bobrowski. As a Polish aristocrat, Conrad's cultural background was Western, and he spoke and read considerably in French. But his father, himself a poet and a dramatist, had been an admirer of English literature, and so as a child Conrad read Shakespeare and Dickens in translation. When he lived alone with his father he was always reading or day-dreaming and developed a passion for travel and adventure. He did not take to the formal schooling he received after his father's death, and as early as 1872 began to beg his uncle to be allowed to go to sea. He was finally given permission to do so when he was seventeen, although his family resented his becoming an ordinary sailor and his apparent rejection of his cultural and social background. He left Poland for Marseilles and for four years led an adventurous life – not only at sea. On his second voyage he seems to have been involved in illegal activities in a Latin-American country, and this later provided material for his great novel *Nostromo*. In Marseilles he helped to smuggle guns to the Spanish Carlists (the supporters of Don Carlos VII) and had a love affair with a beautiful

Basque adventuress, which ended with his attempted suicide. These experiences were later recalled in his novel *The Arrow of Gold* (1919).

Much has been made of Conrad's subsequent transfer from the French to the British merchant navy, because it led eventually to his becoming an English novelist. He was twenty-one when he first came to England and knew very little English then. He taught himself the language, and spent the next fifteen to twenty years at sea, rising from the lowest rank to become a captain. He travelled frequently to the Far East (where many of his stories are set) as well as to India and Australia. In 1886 he became a British citizen.

Although Conrad acknowledged his debt to the French writer Maupassant (1850–93), he was exasperated by the rumour that he had hesitated between French and English when he started writing. He made a point of refuting this story, writing: 'English was for me neither a matter of choice nor adoption . . . there was adoption; but it was I who was adopted by the genius of the language . . . its very idioms . . . had a direct action on my temperament and fashioned my still plastic character'. Although his first published novel, *Almayer's Folly*, was not published until 1895, it seems that Conrad tried his hand at writing stories as early as 1886. The 'tales of hearsay' that all sailors tell helped to shape his technique as a novelist, though from the first Conrad was less interested in events as such than in their impact on characters and in the view of reality they revealed.

In 1890 he went to the Belgian Congo, as a result of which his health was permanently impaired. This contributed to his giving up the sea a few years later, a decision confirmed by his marriage in 1896 to an English girl sixteen years younger than himself. His marriage was a happy one; his wife was good-natured and competent and provided the emotional stability he needed.

Conrad's adventures were now all of the imagination. He wrote slowly, partly by temperament, partly because English was an acquired language; this also made for the unconventionality of his writing. Nevertheless, he produced thirty-one books and a large number of letters. In his early novels and stories, *The Nigger of the Narcissus* (1897), *Lord Jim* (1900), and *Typhoon* (1903), he drew largely on his own experience at sea. This was soon after the first successes of Kipling (1865–1936) when interest in the remote parts of the Empire grew among British people. For a long time, however, Conrad's audience was limited, for he was more than a master of exotic scenes and narratives. The psychological complexity and technical subtleties of his stories sometimes put off his readers. He therefore lived modestly, but had a distinguished group of friends including H.G. Wells (1866–1946), John Galsworthy (1867–1933), and Ford Madox Ford (1873–

1939) with whom he had endless discussions on literary technique. The two artists collaborated in the writing of two novels, *The Inheritors* (1901) and *Romance* (1902). With the great novels that followed his early period Conrad became a master of what is called 'indirect narration', which consists of presenting information in bits and pieces and from different points of view. *Nostromo* (1904) is the story of a revolution in a Latin-American republic and of a theft of a cargo of silver. *The Secret Agent* (1907) is based on the attempt of an anarchist to blow up Greenwich Observatory in 1894 in order to rouse British indignation against the Nihilists. In *Under Western Eyes* (1911), the most Slavic of his novels, Conrad created a memorable character in Razumov, a conspirator turned informer.

Success at last came to Conrad with a novel called *Chance* (1913), ironically not one of his best. His next novel, *Victory* (1915), has the same romantic tone as *Chance* and presents one of Conrad's favourite themes, emotional isolation. In *The Shadow-line* (1917), written in the symbolist manner of his early stories (like *The Secret Sharer*), he presents a positive character, the antithesis of many a negative personality in the earlier novels. Conrad's later books *The Rescue* (1920) and *The Rover* (1923) are generally considered as inferior to his best work. He died of a heart attack in 1924 while writing a novel about Napoleon's return from Elba.

Though it took some time for the full genius of Conrad to be recognised, he himself knew exactly what he was doing, and that in its conception his work was ahead of its time. He wrote:

> I am *modern*, and I would rather recall Wagner the musician and Rodin the sculptor who both had to starve a little in their day . . . they had to suffer for being 'new' . . . My work . . . has the solid basis of definite intention . . . in its essence it is action . . . nothing but action – action observed, felt and interpreted with an absolute truth to my sensations (which are the basis of art in literature) – action of human beings that will bleed to a prick, and are moving in a visible world.

Conrad's journey to the Congo

At the beginning of *Heart of Darkness* Marlow, the narrator, says to his listeners: 'to understand the effect of [my experience in the Congo] you ought to know how I got there, what I saw, how I went up that river' (p.11). Conrad's experience was very similar to Marlow's. Like him, as a young boy, he had a passion for map-gazing and had exclaimed while looking at the blank space in Central Africa where the big River Congo flows: 'When I grow up I will go there' (p.11). He was given to day-dreaming about Africa and wrote about it later in

Last Essays (1926):

> My imagination could depict to itself there worthy, adventurous and devoted men, nibbling at the edges, attacking from north and south and east and west, conquering a bit of truth here and a bit of truth there, and sometimes swallowed up by the mystery their hearts were so persistently set on unveiling.

This passage may be the older man's interpretation of what he imagined, for it combined the mature Conrad's idealistic view of exploration with the realisation that the explorer conquers truth as much as land and may be destroyed by his discoveries.

In 1889 Conrad was in much the same position as his character Marlow, having 'just returned to London after a lot of Indian Ocean, Pacific, China Seas – a regular dose of the East . . . and I was loafing about, hindering you fellows in your work and invading your homes, just as though I had got a heavenly mission to civilise you' (p.11). He was in search of a command, and it may well be also that he saw a map in a shop window in Fleet Street and was reminded of his boyhood dreams of visiting the blank space in Central Africa, although by then 'It had become a place of darkness' (p.12). Again, like Marlow, he 'set the women to work – to get a job' (p.12) in the Congo – actually his aunt Marguerite Poradowska, who had connections with the 'Société Anonyme Belge pour le Commerce du Haut Congo'. The Congo Free State was at that time the personal property of King Leopold II of Belgium. The 'Société', though nominally independent, was administered by a collaborator of the King, Captain Albert Thys, to whom Conrad applied. His interview with Thys is briefly evoked in *Heart of Darkness* where the Captain is referred to as 'an impression of plumpness in a frock-coat' (p.15). Conrad was appointed to replace a Captain Freiesleben (Fresleven in the novel).

He left from Bordeaux in the second week of May 1890 taking with him what he had written of *Almayer's Folly*. His impressions of his voyage down the coast have been recorded in *Heart of Darkness* and are analysed below. What is certain is that on the voyage out disillusionment was already setting in. He was appalled by what he discovered at the company's station at Matadi, as is clear from his creation of what he calls 'the grove of death' in the novel. In Marlow's walk to the Central Station he has also given a fairly close rendering of his own expedition; and, like Marlow, he found upon arrival that the boat he was to command, the *Florida*, had been sunk a few days before. He did not wait two months for the ship to be repaired, however, but sailed the next day on the *Roi des Belges* as second in command to Captain Koch, whom he relieved for a few days when the latter was ill.

The *Roi des Belges* travelled up-river to Stanley Falls in order to relieve an agent called Klein, who was seriously ill and (like Kurtz in *Heart of Darkness*) died on the way back. Kurtz was actually called Klein in the original draft (*kurz* and *klein* mean 'short' and 'small' in German). Whether the real agent served as a model for Kurtz or not matters less than the fact that he represented a type of white man frequently to be met in Africa at the time. Otto Lütken, a Danish captain who worked for eight years in the Congo and wrote approvingly of *Heart of Darkness* (though he pointed out that there *were* admirable white men in the Congo) had this to say about Kurtz: 'It is in the picture Conrad draws of Kurtz . . . that his authorship rises supreme. The man is lifelike and convincing – heavens, how I know him! I have met one or two "Kurtzs" in my time in Africa, and I can see him now.'

Since the beginning of his voyage Conrad's isolation had grown, particularly on the *Roi des Belges*, for he did not get on at all with the company's acting director, Camille Delcommune. After his return to Kinshassa (the Central Station) he was preparing for a ten-month expedition to be led by Alexandre Delcommune, the director's brother, but felt that the director might not keep the promise made to him in Brussels – that Conrad would command the boat on which the expedition was to leave. To his aunt he wrote at the time: 'Everything is repellent to me. Men and things; but especially men. And I too am repellent to them'. His health was also bad; he had discovered that fever and dysentery, rather than the romantic picture of exploration of his youth, was the more common lot of men in Africa. When he realised that he would not receive the command he returned home.

Conrad's four months in the Congo affected both his health and his outlook on life. Of course, they alone cannot be held responsible for Conrad's pessimism and gloomy disposition. He once said to his friend Edward Garnett 'Before the Congo I was a mere animal', by which he meant that he lacked the understanding of existence and the maturity every man ought to attain. His Congo experience put an end to his career as a sailor but made Conrad the artist.

A note on the text

Heart of Darkness was first serialised in *Blackwood's Magazine* from February to April 1899, and then in *Living Age* from 18 June to 4 August 1900. It was first published in book form in 1902 together with *Youth* (as the title story) and *The End of the Tether*. It was re-published in the Uniform Edition of the *Works of Joseph Conrad* (22 vols., Dent, London, 1923–8) with an Author's Note to each volume. It was re-issued in the Collected Edition of the *Works of Joseph Conrad* (Dent, London, 1946–54). These Notes refer to pages in the Penguin Books Edition, Penguin Books, Harmondsworth, 1977.

Part 2

Summaries
of HEART OF DARKNESS

A general summary

In the Thames estuary five men sit on board the *Nellie*, a cruising boat. One is the nameless first narrator of the novel, who introduces his four companions: there is the Director of Companies (their captain and host); a lawyer; an accountant; and finally Marlow, a seaman (who, in several works by Conrad, relates his experiences or, as in *Lord Jim*, comments on the adventurous life of another man). While they are waiting for the tide to turn, Marlow tells the others of an experience he once had in Africa.

As a child he was fascinated by the River Congo (unnamed in the story). His childhood dream materialised when he obtained the command of a steamboat to travel up that river. He first went to Brussels (also unnamed) to visit the headquarters of the company that sponsored his journey. The death-like atmosphere of the city and of the company headquarters, together with the weird behaviour of the people he met there, seemed to him ominous signs. He was, moreover, made uncomfortable by the realisation that he was looked upon as an emissary of light. His uneasiness grew during the journey to Africa, which gave him a first glimpse into the colonialist enterprise.

Marlow's suspicions were confirmed on reaching the first or Outer Station on the river. His first view was of black men made to work for an apparently useless purpose, or being too weak to work and simply left to die. Marlow's horror was matched only by his surprise when he saw a white man, the company's chief accountant, elegantly and meticulously attired, clearly unaware of the surroundings in which he kept the company's books 'in apple-pie order'. The accountant was the first to tell Marlow about Kurtz, the first-class agent he would meet in the interior.

On reaching the Central Station, the next stage in his journey, Marlow was met with the disappointing news that the steamer he was to command had sunk, her bottom torn off as the manager had suddenly attempted to make for the Inner Station without waiting for him. Here Marlow also heard about Kurtz, though no longer with admiration but with resentment and fear. He set to work immediately to repair his boat but couldn't do much without rivets, which took two months to arrive from the Outer Station. Meanwhile a band of explorers headed by the manager's uncle arrived at the Central Station. These did not even pretend to have come on a philanthropic mission; they talked unashamedly of the riches they could extract from the country. One night Marlow overheard a conversation between the manager and his uncle which gave him to understand that the manager was doing his best to delay relieving Kurtz, lying very ill at the Inner Station, in the hope that nature would remove this undesirable rival.

Three months after his arrival at the Central Station, Marlow at last left with the manager and a few pilgrims for the Inner Station, which it took them another two months to reach. In all those months Marlow's curiosity about Kurtz had turned into a sense of growing expectation at the prospect of meeting this man who, in his rival's own words, was 'an emissary of pity, and science, and progress' (p.36). On the way up-river Marlow keenly felt the power of attraction of the wilderness but was prevented from going ashore by the need to be attentive to his work.

With difficulty they reached the Inner Station, where they were welcomed by a young Russian dressed like a harlequin. While the manager and a few pilgrims went on shore, the harlequin came on board and confessed to Marlow his unbounded admiration for Kurtz's eloquence and ideas. He told Marlow in confidence that Kurtz had ordered the attack on the steamboat. Directing his field-glass towards Kurtz's house, Marlow realised that the knobs on the poles of the fence were actually dried human heads. It so horrified him that he refused to hear more from the harlequin about the rites and ceremonies staged by the natives in honour of Kurtz.

Meanwhile Kurtz was being carried on board, a very ill and emaciated man, a mere voice, as Marlow now insists, but a still deep, vibrating and eloquent one. He was followed to the shore by a crowd of natives. A magnificent woman, Kurtz's black mistress, appeared and raised her arms in a dramatic gesture that seemed to release swift shadows before she disappeared again. Shortly afterwards, the manager's unfavourable comments on Kurtz drove Marlow to side with the latter, glad to have at least a 'choice of nightmares'.

After midnight, when all were asleep on board, Marlow looked into the cabin where Kurtz had been lying and saw that he was not there. He did not betray him, but went on shore alone after him and managed to bring him back by outwitting him and breaking the spell that drew him to the wilderness. As they journeyed away from the 'heart of darkness', Kurtz discoursed eloquently about his ideas and his plans almost until the moment of his death, unaware of the discrepancy between his words and his actions. He gave Marlow a report he had written on the 'Suppression of Savage Customs', having forgotten all about his own postcript, 'Exterminate all the brutes!' (p.72). Only at the very last instant did he seem to pass judgement on his life when he cried out 'the horror! the horror!' (p.100).

Marlow himself nearly died of fever but came back to Brussels, the wiser for his experience and irritated by the ignorance and complacency of the people he met in the street. He was visited by several acquaintances and relatives of Kurtz, who each gave him a different picture of the 'great' man. He fulfilled what he saw as a last duty to Kurtz by visiting his Intended (his fiancée), about whom he had heard so much from Kurtz himself. As he entered the house towards evening, his vision of Kurtz as a voracious shadow seemed to enter with him. The impressions of darkness and light that Marlow gathered from the drawing-room converged on the girl, for she was dressed in black and had a lofty forehead on which the light took refuge as the room grew darker. In the ensuing conversation Marlow was made uneasy once more, then desperate and even angry by the girl's unquestioned admiration for Kurtz's greatness and eloquence, her deep conviction that 'he died as he lived'. He did not undeceive her, however, nor take away the 'great and saving illusion' that sustained her. When asked what Kurtz's last words were, he actually lied and said that his last words had been her name.

Marlow's tale over, the first narrator concludes the narrative. The Thames which, at the beginning of the novel, he saw flowing in 'tranquil dignity' crowded with memories of the feats of British conquerors, he now sees flowing 'sombre under an overcast sky . . . into the heart of an immense darkness' (p.111).

Detailed summaries

Because of its complexity we can consider *Heart of Darkness* as a short novel rather than a long short story. It consists of three fairly long chapters. The first one ends just after the arrival at the Central Station of the El Dorado Expedition, whose rapaciousness shocks Marlow and makes him wonder how, by contrast, Kurtz will put his moral ideas into practice when in power. The second chapter ends just after the rescue party reaches the Inner Station and the harlequin asserts to Marlow that Kurtz 'has enlarged [his] mind' (p.78).

It is possible, however, to divide the narrative into a series of episodes which roughly represent significant stages in Marlow's expedition. Naturally, this division is not Conrad's but has been devised to help the student in his close reading of the text. The full meaning of each episode can only be assessed by keeping in mind the novel as a whole, for the narrative is full of parallels, contrasts and echoes.

Chapter 1, Episode 1: From the beginning to 'I felt as though . . . I were about to set off for the centre of the earth' (p.18).

The novel begins with a description of the Thames Estuary at the end of the day. The light over the estuary contrasts with the gloom over London, and the five men on board the *Nellie* are in a silent, pensive mood. The first narrator feels the 'spirit of the place' prevailing in their present environment, and meditates on Britain's past conquerors and explorers – men who, starting from that same estuary, contributed to the wealth and fame of their country and sometimes carried the torch of civilisation to the ends of the earth. As if he could read his thoughts Marlow suddenly says: 'And this also . . . has been one of the dark places of the earth' (p.7). He was not thinking of Britain's glorious past but of its dark ages when it was invaded by the Romans, who would have been fascinated by its wilderness. He insists that, whereas the Romans were mere robbers, contemporary colonisers are saved by efficiency and the 'idea' behind colonialism. After a short pause Marlow introduces his story as if it had no connection with colonial expeditions. He explains that he got his command of a steamer to travel up the Congo through the help of an aunt who knew a high official in the continental company that administered the Congo. He was appointed in replacement of a Dane called Fresleven, speared in retaliation for killing an old village chief with whom he had quarrelled over two hens.

Marlow's first contact with the colonial enterprise begins in Brussels, the city that reminds him of a 'whited sepulchre'. A dead silence prevails in the vicinity of the company headquarters. Marlow is briefly but ceremoniously interviewed in the 'sanctuary' of the company director. This troubles him, though not so much as the presence in the waiting room of two women, one fat and old, the other slim and younger, both knitting black wool uninterruptedly even while introducing people to 'the unknown' (actually the director's office). The company secretary, who has told Marlow he is not such a fool as to go to Africa himself, takes him to a doctor's for the necessary medical examination. The doctor measures Marlow's skull and to his question 'Are you an alienist?' he answers 'Every doctor should be – a little' (p.17). When Marlow goes to say goodbye to his aunt, he realises that she is convinced he is taking the light of civilisation to 'ignorant millions' (p.18). It makes him feel an impostor. He also has a queer feeling that he is about to travel to 'the centre of the earth' (p.18).

COMMENTARY: The first episode presents the development of the novel in a nutshell. As Marlow's story will show, the contrast between light and darkness in the setting conveys a duality also to be found in men and their enterprises. Light is normally associated with civilisation and its ideals, with enlightenment, consciousness and self-knowledge; while darkness usually represents the wilderness, ignorance and evil. We may have the impression at first that Conrad subscribes to this conventional distinction – but he soon undermines it. Whereas the first narrator thinks of the heroic deeds of British conquerors, Marlow sees the Roman invaders, the civilised men of 'very old times', facing a dark and hostile continent. But he also sees them as violent men robbing what they could from the invaded country. This shows that the so-called bringers of light, who faced the darkness of the wilderness, were themselves agents of darkness. Although Marlow asserts that 'we' (which can refer to English colonists or contemporary colonisers in general) are different from the Romans, his definition of colonialism is universal and applies to all colonisers. It stresses the ambivalent nature of colonialism:

> The conquest of the earth, which mostly means the taking it away from those who have a different complexion or slightly flatter noses than ourselves, is not a pretty thing when you look into it too much. What redeems it is the idea only . . . something you can set up, and bow down before, and offer a sacrifice to . . . (p.10)

Marlow's tale so far has several effects. It corrects the first narrator's simple optimism by pointing to the evil of conquest and referring indirectly to the conquered people's view of the matter. It suggests that the colonial expedition, though a national enterprise, is also an ordeal testing the individual man and revealing to him his susceptibility to being fascinated by the 'abomination' of the wilderness and of his own dark instincts. It also gives the reader a sense of the rise and fall of civilisations. The once powerful Roman Empire has disappeared, while Britain, once a dark continent, has built an empire which may one day pass away too.

Marlow's view of Brussels as a 'whited sepulchre' with its connotation of hypocrisy and deadliness, the attitude and allusions of the people he meets there and his aunt's assumption that he is a gifted creature who goes to Africa as a kind of apostle; these sow in him the seed of an as yet undefinable malaise.

NOTES AND GLOSSARY:

the flood had made: the tide had risen

Sir Francis Drake: (c.1543–96) one of the most famous Elizabethan seamen, who commanded the *Golden Hind* on a journey to South America, partly to make discoveries, partly for plunder

Sir John Franklin: (1786–1847) an English admiral and explorer who commanded an expedition to the Northwest Passage on the *Erebus* and the *Terror*

mizzen-mast: the mast aft of the main mast in a ship

Falernian wine: from a district of Campania in Southern Italy. This wine was highly appreciated by the Romans

Ravenna: a large Roman base in northern Italy

Whited Sepulchre: a phrase used by Christ to denounce the hypocrisy of scribes and Pharisees (see the Bible, Matthew 23:27)

there was a vast amount of red: red was the colour of British overseas possessions on the map

Ave! . . . Morituri te salutant: (Latin) Hail! . . . Those who are about to die salute you

Plato: (428–348BC) a Greek philosopher

du calme, du calme: *(French)* 'keep cool' or 'don't get excited'

adieu: goodbye

Chapter 1, Episode 2: From 'I left in a French steamer' (p.18) to 'He is waiting!' (p.30).

Marlow travels to Africa on a French steamer. He is fascinated by the coast of the African continent which presents itself to him as an enigma, an impression enhanced by the sense of isolation he experiences among men with whom he has nothing in common. Only the noisy surf and an occasional boat paddled by sturdy negroes restore his sense of reality and make him feel he is in contact with something meaningful and real. Once they see a man-of-war firing insanely and incomprehensively into an apparently empty continent, although someone assures Marlow they are firing at 'enemies'. After several stops at trading posts with farcical names, they reach the mouth of the Congo and Marlow boards a steamer that will take him up-river to the company's Outer Station.

The captain of the boat, a young Swede, expresses his bitter contempt for the 'government chaps' and tells Marlow about a countryman of his who committed suicide shortly after reaching the Congo. When they arrive at the Outer Station, Marlow comes into contact for the first time with the reality of the colonial exploitation.

The land itself is being devastated by repeated blastings, even of areas that are not in the way of the projected railway. Black slaves, chained to each other with an iron collar on their necks, carry baskets of earth from one place to another. When Marlow walks down to the river to keep out of their way, he comes upon a nightmarish scene: the ghostly figures of dying natives – overworked, starved and too weak to move – recline in the shade. Marlow feels he has 'stepped into the gloomy circle of some inferno' (p.24). 'Horror-struck', he climbs towards the station and meets a white man so elegantly and spotlessly dressed in white that Marlow takes him for a sort of vision. This is the chief accountant, whom Marlow sincerely admires and respects for what he has accomplished; the preservation of his impeccable appearance and the perfect keeping of his books in the midst of the surrounding confusion and the 'demoralisation of the land'. The accountant, however, cannot stand the groans of a dying man left in his office to await a passage home, and when some natives in the yard are too noisy he comments that 'one comes to hate those savages – hate them to the death' (p.27).

After ten days Marlow starts on a two-hundred-mile trek towards the Central Station. Already at the Outer Station Marlow foresaw that in the Congo he would 'become acquainted with a flabby, pretending, weak-eyed devil of a rapacious and pitiless folly' (p.23). Arriving at the Central Station after a trying journey, he sees immediately that this 'flabby devil' rules the place. He is told that the steamer he is to command has sunk and that the manager is expecting him.

COMMENTARY: It is clear from the beginning that Marlow's journey calls for several interpretations and that the narrative develops on two planes, the actual and the symbolical. Marlow's very concrete rendering of his journey also evokes an expedition into the psyche. To give but one example of the double meaning of the narrative, when Marlow steps 'into the gloomy circle of some inferno' at the Outer Station, the disturbing shadows he comes upon are exploited men but can also be seen as so many inner selves.

The expedition is a personal ordeal for Marlow and his reactions to what he discovers are an essential part of the narrative. His first impression is that the white man is an intruder in Africa. He violates the country, while trade (mainly a scramble for ivory) only brings despair and death in its wake. The first negroes Marlow sees on the edge of the continent are full of vitality, but as he goes in he meets first men reduced to slavery, then mere shadows left to die like animals. The darkness of the 'inferno' at the Outer Station is the reality the whites have brought with them, and the light of civilisation subsists only in appearances: for example in the light attire of the accountant and his devotion to the outer forms (his impeccable accounts) rather than the values of civilisation. The whites' work in Africa, moreover, appears to be utterly useless or inefficient.

Marlow's matter-of-fact tone enhances the impression of horror created by his words. It also adds to the irony which pervades his narrative and arises from the discrepancy between the apparent commonplaceness of some of his statements and the reality they convey. When, for example, he comes across a vast artificial hole and wonders why it has been dug, he declares 'It might have been connected with the philanthropic desire of giving the criminals something to do' (p.24). The juxtaposition of 'philanthropic desire' with 'criminals' expresses indirectly but forcefully the monstrosity of the whites' enterprise.

NOTES AND GLOSSARY:

railway-truck: when Conrad went to the Congo, a railway was being built from Matadi to Kinshassa in order to by-pass the thirty-two rapids in the lower Congo which made navigation extremely difficult

raw-matter: it is the savages whom Marlow calls 'raw-matter' because of the way in which they are being treated

Inferno: a place of torment and suffering that suggests Hell. Also the title of one of the books in the *Divina Commedia* (1310–21), the great Christian poem written by the Italian poet Dante Alighieri (1265–1321)

a bit of white worsted: a piece of white fabric made of worsted yarns

a propitiatory act: an act intended to appease or conciliate a higher authority or power

a first-class agent: this does not mean an excellent agent – although the accountant would clearly consider it fitting to apply this epithet to Kūrtz – but one of higher rank

---

Chapter 1, Episode 3: From 'I did not see the real significance' (p.30) to the end of Chapter 1 (p.44).

Immediately after his arrival at the Central Station, Marlow is received by the manager who does not even invite him to sit down after his twenty-mile walk in the jungle that day. The manager inspires un-easiness, not because of his superiority, but because (as Marlow soon discovers) 'there was nothing within him' and he was once heard to say ' "Men who come out here should have no entrails" ' (p.31). This seems to be the case with the brickmaker, a first-class agent supposed to be making bricks, although none are to be seen around the station. Marlow suspects that if he poked his forefinger through him he 'would find nothing inside but a little loose dirt, maybe' (p.37). The other white men at the station seem equally aimless, their only concern being for ivory, a word ringing constantly in the air. Because they seem to be praying to it and carry long staves, Marlow calls them 'faithless pilgrims' (p.33).

On the morrow of his arrival Marlow sets down to work to repair his boat, but he cannot do so for lack of rivets. He knows there are plenty of them at the Outer Station and that a messenger travels there from the Central Station every week, but he will have to wait about two months before he gets any, and he is surprised that the manager proved to be right in his prediction when he told him the steamer would take three months to repair. Meanwhile a fire breaks out at the Central Station, and an obviously innocent African is cruelly beaten up for it. While others ineffectually try to stop the fire (one pilgrim even carries a pail with a hole in its bottom) Marlow starts a conversation with the brickmaker, who invites him to his hut. He soon realises, however, that the brickmaker is trying to pump him about his acquaintances in Brussels. When the brickmaker gets angry at Marlow's failure to respond, the latter gets up and only then notices a small painting done by Kurtz 'representing a woman, draped and blindfolded, carrying a lighted torch' (p.36).

Marlow, who has already been struck by the manager's reference to Kurtz during their first conversation, asks the brickmaker outright who this Mr Kurtz is. He receives an ambivalent answer, being told in a dutiful yet sceptical tone that Kurtz is 'an emissary of pity, and science, and progress' (p.36), the kind of man who is needed to serve the civilising cause of Europe. Kurtz is a representative of the new 'gang of virtue' and the people who sent him are the same who recommended Marlow. The latter now understands why he is looked upon with suspicion by the jealous manager and pilgrims. He nevertheless asks the brickmaker to help him to get rivets and, back on his boat, dances like a lunatic at the thought of getting them. The rivets, however, do not come so soon. Instead, the Eldorado Exploring Expedition, a 'gang' of greedy exploiters led by the manager's uncle, comes to the station.

COMMENTARY: In this section Marlow introduces two *leitmotives* (recurring ideas) of his narrative. One is that 'out there there were no external checks' (p.31) on one's behaviour. The other is that work alone can help one keep a hold 'on the redeeming facts of life' (p.33). This becomes particularly important in the other two chapters when Marlow, like Kurtz, is tempted to give in to the wilderness. At this stage it is clear that the main source of temptation for the white man is ivory and that the pilgrims have made a god of it. Marlow is not tempted by ivory but he is greatly impressed by the silent powerfulness of the primeval forest which, like the African coast before, presents itself as an enigma to him. The forest is where ivory is to be found and the place where Kurtz lives. Although Marlow does not know yet what he will find in the heart of darkness, a link is unobtrusively suggested between men's lust for ivory and the forest as a place where they are tempted to yield to their lower instincts. Marlow can therefore ask 'could we handle this dumb thing, or would it handle us?' (p.38). This question anticipates the more specific one he later asks about Kurtz: 'Everything belonged to him . . . the thing was to know what he belonged to' (p.70). So far, however, what Marlow has heard about Kurtz from the accountant, the manager and the brickmaker has merely made him curious about him. Indeed, all he has seen of the white man's behaviour in Africa represents one kind of evil or another: lunatic or futile action, inefficiency, ruthless exploitation of the natives and, at the Central Station, hollowness and pretence. What is Kurtz really like, who is presented as an idealist even by those who fear him?

NOTES AND GLOSSARY:

Jack: an ill-mannered fellow

assegais: slender hardwood spears

there is something . . . in the world allowing one man to steal a horse while another must not look at a halter: a certain way of coveting a halter is far worse than stealing the horse itself

papier-maché Mephistopheles: an unreal, insubstantial devil

Huntley and Palmers: a well-known biscuit making company

ichthyosaurus: a prehistoric reptile

El Dorado: a fabulously wealthy city or country that sixteenth-century explorers thought existed in South America

---

Chapter 2, Episode 1: From 'One evening as I was lying flat on the deck of my steamboat' (p.44) to 'beyond my power of meddling' (p.55).

One evening Marlow overhears a conversation between the manager and his uncle. They are talking about Kurtz and both hope that the jungle, which kills off so many people, will also remove him from the manager's way to success.

At last Marlow's steamboat is repaired and he leaves with the manager and a few pilgrims. As he progresses from the Central to the Inner Station, Marlow feels as if he were 'travelling back to the earliest beginnings of the world' (p.48). He is now penetrating the unknown territory of the wilderness, and the philosophic comments the journey elicits from him remind us that it is also a metaphor for an inner exploration.

As he comes into contact with a world untrammelled by the trappings of civilisation, Marlow's first overwhelming impression is that an inner truth is hidden in both nature and men. He senses the truth of nature in its potent and mysterious stillness (p.49) even though the earth is here 'a thing monstrous and free' (p.51). The enthusiastic outbreak of the prehistoric men on the shore as they watch the passing steamboat is unadulterated reaction: 'joy, fear, sorrow, devotion, valour, rage', what Marlow calls 'truth stripped of its cloak of time' (p.52). He asserts that in order to face that truth man needs an 'inborn strength' and a 'deliberate belief' which he opposes to mere principles. These, to him, are like 'rags that would fly off at the first good shake' (p.52). Marlow's own deliberate belief seems to be in the efficiency of work, which helps him resist the appeal of the wilderness. We are here reminded of his earlier assertion: 'I like what is in the work – the chance to find yourself. Your own reality' (p.41).

This capacity to assert oneself through work is what Marlow means when he says 'I have a voice, too' (p.52). He soon finds support for his belief when he discovers an abandoned hut on the shore. A white man has left there a pile of wood for Marlow's steamboat and a message 'approach cautiously'. This can only refer to the Inner Station. Near the entrance of the hut Marlow finds a book called *An enquiry into some Points of Seamanship* by an old naval man, and recognises in it 'a singleness of intention, an honest concern for the right way of going to work'. This section ends with Marlow's conjectures about his forthcoming meeting with Kurtz. He now feels that his penetration into the heart of darkness is exclusively a progress towards Kurtz.

COMMENTARY: The assertion by the manager's uncle that 'Anything – anything can be done in this country' (p.46), an illustration of Marlow's conviction that 'out there there were no external checks', as well as the uncle's appeal 'to the lurking death, to the hidden evil, to the profound darkness of the [land's] heart' (p.47) show that evil in nature is brought out by man and reflects the evil in his own heart. It would be a mistake and a simplification to consider the heart of darkness itself as a metaphor for evil. Its effect in this passage is to make Marlow think about man in general and the respective meanings of white and black cultures.

Man, particularly the white man with his technological achievement, is still very small compared to grandiose nature as witness 'the little begrimed steamboat' crawling 'like a sluggish beetle' between 'the high walls' (p.50) of the jungle. Moreover, just as the white man must be in the natives' eyes 'an insoluble mystery from the sea' (p.23), so the black man is an enigma for the white explorer: 'The prehistoric man was cursing us, praying to us, welcoming us – who could tell? We were cut off from the comprehension of our surroundings' (p.51). In effect, Marlow is discovering that one type of man is not superior to another, but that each is a mystery for the other. The white man, however, can understand what he shares with prehistoric man if he is prepared to face humanity's past in himself: 'The mind of man is capable of any-thing – because everything is in it, all the past as well as all the future' (p.51). Man can face what he discovers in the prehistoric world with what Marlow calls 'inborn strength' and 'deliberate belief', which clearly imply authenticity, that is, faithfulness to what one is and awareness of one's capacities. The fireman, like Marlow, is prevented from going ashore 'for a howl and a dance' (p.52) by the task in hand, but he is forced to do work unnatural to him and which he does not understand. Men (whether white or black) faced with the incompre-hensible and lacking 'inborn strength' are less capable of restraint in a situation of strain than the cannibals, 'Fine fellows . . . men one could work with' (p.50).

NOTES AND GLOSSARY:
tight-rope: a rope stretched taut on which acrobats perform
half-a-crown a tumble: the price an acrobat gets for each acrobatic feat. Half-a-crown was worth two shillings and sixpence, one-eighth of the pound sterling, before decimal currency was introduced

---

Chapter 2, Episode 2: From 'Towards the evening of the second day' (p.55) to 'Here, give me some tobacco . . .' (p.68).

The manager further delays their approach to the Inner Station but this time Marlow must admit that to proceed in the dark would be dangerous. Marlow describes the atmosphere prevailing on the river in the vicinity of the Inner Station. The bush seems to be frozen into an unnatural state of trance, which makes men suspect that they are deaf as well as blind when night falls. In the morning a thick fog, at once 'blind' (p.60) and 'more blinding than the night' (p.56) envelops the whole area, and Marlow finds it extremely difficult to progress on the narrow reach of the river obstructed with dangerous snags. A very loud cry, to Marlow an expression of extreme and unrestrained grief, pierces the fog. He compares the reaction of the whites to this suddenly-revealed presence of natives on the shore with that of the cannibals on board. The whites are very nervous. On the contrary the blacks, who are also strangers in this area and as unfamiliar with it as the whites, remain calm and self-controlled although they ask Marlow to catch their hidden opponents for them to eat.

This reminds Marlow that the natives on the boat have not received any food for weeks. They have been forced to throw overboard the rotten hippo-meat that was their sole provision for the journey, and receive three pieces of brass wire every week to buy food which is not to be had anyway. Marlow meditates on the enigmatic source of the cannibals' self-restraint and 'inborn strength', for he is convinced that there is no more exasperating and ferocious torment than hunger. By contrast, the only restraint the manager is capable of is hypocrisy for he now declares 'I would be desolated if anything should happen to Mr Kurtz before we came up' (p.60).

Contrary to Marlow's assertion that they would not do so, the natives on shore attack the boat, although Marlow considers their action as a protective one, an attempt at repulse on the part of desperate men. The incomers are shot at with arrows which, to Marlow, seem harmless. The pilgrims, however, lose their self-control and blindly unload their Winchesters on to the bush. So does the black helmsman (spoiled by so-called civilisation, like the fireman). He opens the shutter of the pilot house (previously closed by Marlow) and fires. He is speared and dies with a familiar, then a questioning, glance at Marlow. The latter quickly pulls the boat's steam-whistle. The attack is checked instantly and another wail of despair arises from the bush. While Marlow anxiously changes his shoes, which are full of the helmsman's blood, he experiences a keen disappointment at the thought that Kurtz might also be dead. He realises that he thinks of Kurtz as 'a voice' and that he has been looking forward to a talk with Kurtz throughout the journey. He also realises that his sorrow at possibly missing that talk is as extravagant as the natives' cry of despair.

COMMENTARY: In this passage the travellers on the steamboat are further isolated from anything they know. The reaction of black and white men to their disturbing position is clearly not a question of race, since both the pilgrims and the uprooted helmsman are incapable of restraint. Marlow is efficient and shows great presence of mind in keeping the boat clear of snags and pulling the steam-whistle which frightens their assailants. The manager (who has done his best to delay their arrival at the Inner Station, first by sinking the steamboat, then by not letting Marlow have rivets to repair it) is sincere when he says he would be sorry if Kurtz died before they came, because he wants to keep up appearances. Towards both the natives and Kurtz he is determined to keep up what Marlow called earlier the 'sentimental' (p.10) or 'philanthropic pretence' (p.35) but there is no end to which he will not go to ensure his power over the colony in opposition to Kurtz. By emphasising this point in a passage which, by comparison, shows the admirable restraint of the starving cannibals, Marlow suggests that the whites are guilty of an uncontrolled and devouring appetite for material riches (ivory) which is cannibalistic in nature. We shall see that an extreme form of it is to be found in Kurtz. The self-restraint of the cannibals remains a mystery to Marlow. But he notices that the helmsman, who, like the white man in Africa, has lost the support of his community by doing an incomprehensible job for the whites, dies utterly bewildered. The as yet unexplained grief of the natives on shore, and Marlow's own grief at the thought that he might be too late to hear Kurtz, are a significant comment on this man's power of eloquence. Marlow increases his listeners' (and the reader's) suspense about Kurtz by presenting it as an ambivalent gift: 'the gift of expression, the bewildering, the illuminating, the most exalted and the most contemptible, the pulsating stream of light, or the deceitful flow from the heart of an impenetrable darkness' (p.68).

NOTES AND GLOSSARY:
Martini-Henry: a type of rifle
Winchester: also a type of rifle, named after the manufacturer

---

Chapter 2, Episode 3: From 'There was a pause of profound stillness' (p.68) to the end of Chapter 2 (p.78).

A deep sigh from one of his listeners stops Marlow in his narrative. The interruption makes him aware of his listeners' possible perplexity in reaction to his upsetting tale. After a short pause he launches into a fairly long digression (from p.68 to p.73). Its main import is a comparison between the situation of the white man in his own society and that of Kurtz in the jungle. In his own environment the white man is protected from his own worst instincts by the butcher, who satisfies his appetite, and the policeman, who keeps alive his fear of scandal, of the gallows and of the lunatic asylum. When he is deprived of these supports in the 'utter solitude' (p.70) of the jungle, man must fall back upon his 'own innate strength' and his 'capacity for faithfulness' (p.70) (another expression for 'deliberate belief').

Anticipating his meeting with Kurtz and the impression the latter made on him, Marlow asserts that in the solitude of the jungle Kurtz has been consumed by the wilderness outside and within himself. 'He had taken a high seat amongst the devils of the land' (p.70) and was incapable of restraining his lust for possession. Marlow adds that all Europe had contributed to the making of Kurtz and that he had been asked by the International Society for the Suppression of Savage Customs to write a report for its guidance. Marlow has read the report, which was obviously written before Kurtz himself began to preside over 'unspeakable rites' (p.71) offered to him. The report ominously started with the assertion that whites must necessarily appear to savages as supernatural beings. Yet Marlow confesses that he was greatly impressed by the report and Kurtz's 'burning noble words';

until he reached the postscript, clearly written much later, which read 'Exterminate all the brutes' (p.72). Reflecting on this inner contradiction, Marlow concludes that Kurtz was not worth the helmsman's life lost for him.

This allusion to his helmsman who, Marlow comments, lacked restraint 'just like Kurtz' (p.73), brings him back to the main strand of his narrative. He shocks the pilgrims by promptly throwing the helmsman's body overboard before his cannibal woodcutters are tempted by him. Shortly afterwards they reach the Inner Station and Marlow notices carved balls ornamenting posts around the house. They are welcomed by a funny white man dressed all in patches, who reminds Marlow of a harlequin. He has a boyish face 'overcast one moment and bright the next' (p.76). He is a Russian, the man who prepared wood for Marlow. He calls the natives 'simple people' and confirms that it was the steam-whistle that frightened them. He expresses the greatest admiration for Kurtz, though from the first he appears to hide something from Marlow. But he keeps repeating that Kurtz 'has enlarged [his] mind'.

COMMENTARY: The effect of Marlow's long digression and of the contrast he draws between the white man's living conditions in Europe and in Africa is to warn the reader that, placed in similar circumstances, any white man might react like Kurtz. Marlow reflects Conrad's pessimism when he suggests that it is not the white man's conscience but his fear of the policeman and of public opinion that keeps him on the straight path. Moreover, it would seem that the 'innate strength' and 'faithfulness' which Marlow so much praises as means of resisting the wilderness only really help man to ignore it, to dig 'unostentatious holes' in which to bury 'dead hippo' (p.71) – a metaphor for the wilderness.

This passage makes clear both Kurtz's dualism and Marlow's own ambivalent reaction to him. Kurtz sees himself as great ('everything belonged to him' (p.70)) but he has in fact been reduced to a mere 'shade', an 'initiated wraith' (p.71). The natives have made a god of him and he looks upon himself in that light too. But the postscript to his report reveals that *he* is a bloodthirsty brute. His conviction of being a superior being and his insatiable hunger for power have led him to behave like a god and to arrogate to himself the right to destroy all those who are different from himself. That all Europe should have contributed to his making is a sign of his representativeness. Marlow's feeling for him is a mixture of admiration for his 'unbounded power of eloquence' (p.72) and of utter contempt. The harlequin's alternating smiles and frowns and his uneasiness present Marlow with another mystery.

NOTES AND GLOSSARY:
harlequin: a quick-witted servant who is a stock character in the *commedia dell'arte*; he usually wears a mask and parti-coloured tights

---

Chapter 3, Episode 1: From 'I looked at him, lost in astonishment' (p.78) to 'Ah, well, it's all over now' (p.88).

Marlow admires the harlequin's resilience and his unreflecting audacity. He envies his glamour and pure spirit of adventure but not his thoughtless admiration for Kurtz. Though the harlequin is reluctant to tell the whole truth, Marlow gradually makes out that after he had no more goods to trade with, Kurtz raided the country for ivory with the help of an inland tribe who had become his unconditional followers and 'adored' him. In spite of the harlequin's entreaty Kurtz had refused to leave the Inner Station while there was still time. The harlequin had nursed him through two illnesses, yet Kurtz had threatened to kill him if he did not relinquish to him (Kurtz) what little ivory he had. This the harlequin found quite justifiable.

While they are talking Marlow has taken his binoculars, and looking at the carved balls ornamenting the fence around Kurtz's house, he suddenly realises they are not ornaments but dried human heads on stakes. To Marlow these show that Kurtz 'lacked restraint in the gratification of his various lusts' and also that he was 'hollow at the core' (p.83). Again, he anticipates what is to come by suggesting that the knowledge of his deficiency came to Kurtz at the very last. Meanwhile, he refuses to hear more of Kurtz's relations with the natives (what he has termed above 'unspeakable rites' [p.71]) and cannot hide his stupefaction from the harlequin, who asserts that the heads on the stakes are those of rebels. The harlequin declares that he himself is a simple man and does not understand the complex temptations to which a great man like Kurtz is apparently liable.

At this juncture, Kurtz himself appears carried on a stretcher. Marlow sees him as a 'phantom' and a 'shadow', an 'animated image of death' with a 'weirdly voracious aspect' (p.85). His voice, however, is still impressive and he manages to restrain the natives who have uttered a shrill cry at his departure and come out of the bush. Kurtz is laid down in one the boat's small cabins, and the manager joins him while Marlow and the Russian look at the shore. A magnificent black woman, whom Marlow describes in some detail, now makes her appearance. She is at once savage and superb. Before disappearing again she throws her arms up in a dramatic gesture and at the same time swift shadows gather around the river and the boat which until then were in the sunshine. The harlequin expresses his hostility towards her. It seems that she dislikes him too and once quarrelled with Kurtz about him but, again, the harlequin can only repeat: 'I don't understand' (p.88).

COMMENTARY: The harlequin prepares Marlow for his meeting with Kurtz. He, too, is an ambivalent character; his youthfulness and extraordinary capacity to survive, together with the efficiency it implies, contrast with his indiscriminate adoration of Kurtz, for he cannot say precisely in what way Kurtz has enriched his life. There is an ironic contrast between his reiterated statements: '[Kurtz] has enlarged my mind' and 'I don't understand'. This reflects as much on the nature of Kurtz's eloquence (beautiful but vague, as Marlow's own judgement shows) as on the harlequin.

Marlow first meets Kurtz just after becoming aware that the ornaments on stakes around his house are human heads and he has commented on Kurtz's hollowness. This seems to contradict an earlier suggestion that, unlike the pilgrims, Kurtz is not hollow because he has at least ideals that can become corrupted. He clearly does not belong to the category of man of whom Marlow said: 'I take it, no fool ever made a bargain for his soul with the devil: the fool is too much of a fool, or the devil too much of a devil' (p.70). Kurtz, however, is hollow in that he lacks the moral capacity to resist the wilderness. He has no moral sense on which to act and is not even aware of the discrepancy between his very real idealism and his actions.

The superb black woman who appears on the shore is clearly an embodiment of the wilderness. But again, we must beware of attributing too simple a symbolism to Marlow's narrative. The tragic sorrow on her face suggests that she does not represent evil, or not that only. Moreover, her effect on Marlow now and at the moment of departure is ambivalent. He is at once repelled by her and full of admiration.

NOTES AND GLOSSARY:
Jupiter:　　　　the chief god in Roman mythology

Chapter 3, Episode 2: From 'At this moment I heard Kurtz's deep voice' (p.88) to 'I could see nothing more for smoke' (p.97).

Marlow's conversation with the harlequin is interrupted by Kurtz's loud protest, behind the curtain of the cabin, that the manager has come to save not him but the ivory; and that in fact it was Kurtz who had to save the manager and his companions from being attacked by Kurtz's resentful native followers. When the manager comes out of the cabin he complains that Kurtz's method is unsound and that the trade will suffer. Marlow's first rejoinder is that Kurtz has 'no method at all' but he checks the manager's exultation at this by asserting that Kurtz is a remarkable man. He is therefore lumped with Kurtz as unsound but finds it a relief from the manager's vile hypocrisy and is glad to have at least 'a choice of nightmares' (p.89). Before leaving the steamboat the harlequin reveals to Marlow that it was Kurtz who ordered the natives to attack it. Because he is concerned about Kurtz's reputation, he warns Marlow against what Kurtz might yet do.

Marlow wakes up shortly after midnight and recalls the harlequin's warning. He perceives that deep within the forest black columnar shapes move around the red gleams of a fire. Marlow is aroused from his half-awakened state by the sudden yells of the natives. Looking into Kurtz's cabin, he realises that it is empty. His reaction is one of 'pure abstract terror' due to the 'moral shock' he has received as if he were confronted with something 'monstrous' (p.92). Marlow, however, does not betray Kurtz. He goes ashore after him recalling (rather irrelevantly, it seems) the knitting old woman in Brussels, and imagining he might be left alone in the jungle. He overtakes Kurtz with whom he fights as with a 'shadow', being aware all the time that if Kurtz chose to make a row they would all be lost. He appeals to Kurtz's pride in what he has achieved in order to break the spell of the wilderness on him, and persuades him to return to the boat. Recalling this episode Marlow is prompted to another short digression, first about the terrible isolation of Kurtz's soul which 'had looked within itself, and . . . had gone mad', then, anticipating again, about the significance of Kurtz's last words. When Kurtz is at last back in his cabin Marlow feels as if he had been carrying half a ton, although the emaciated Kurtz is hardly heavier than a child.

The next day, as they are about to leave, the shore fills with frantic natives whose deep murmurs are like 'some satanic litany'. Kurtz's black mistress is there again. She puts out her arms and shouts something after the boat which is taken up by the crowd. To Marlow's question 'Do you understand this?' (p.96), Kurtz answers with a smile of indefinable meaning 'Do I not?' (p.97). As they leave, Marlow blows the steam-whistle and disperses the natives. Only the superb black woman does not flinch and remains with her arms tragically stretched out after the boat.

COMMENTARY: Another expression of Conrad's pessimism is to be found in Marlow's assertion that he has 'a choice of nightmares' – a choice, that is, between the vile hypocrisy of the manager and the corruption of Kurtz. Marlow's knowledge that Kurtz has ordered the attack on the boat, together with the moral shock he receives when he realises that Kurtz has gone ashore, confirm (if need be) Kurtz's total surrender to his baser instincts. That Marlow should be shocked morally and not just afraid of the very real danger in which they all are emphasises the nature of his quest. It is not just an errand to retrieve Kurtz. His soul is at stake and so is Marlow's. His appeal to Kurtz's pride and egoism also confirms the source of Kurtz's corruption; it is essentially the result of his boundless will-to-power. Yet Marlow does not betray him then or later. Once more he creates suspense, first about the reason of his fidelity to Kurtz, then about Kurtz's last words. By insisting that he does not understand his own behaviour, he stimulates his listeners (and the readers) to reflect on it. Kurtz's assertion that he understands the appeal of the natives and of his black mistress contrasts with the simplicity and bewilderment of the harlequin.

Chapter 3, Episode 3: From 'The brown current ran swiftly' (p.97) to the end.

The boat now travels down-river towards the sea much faster than it did upwards. The pilgrims still look upon Marlow as an associate of Kurtz and this is to some extent justified by the fact that Kurtz talks to Marlow alone, making him the confidant of his great hopes but confirming at the same time the discrepancy between these and the 'hollow sham' (p.98) he has become. His life is fast running out, and it seems that almost to the end he remains self-deceived. However, just before he dies, it is 'as though a veil had been rent' (p.99) and Marlow reads on his face contradictory emotions of pride and ruthless power on one hand, terror and hopeless despair on the other. Kurtz's last moment is one of 'complete knowledge', and he exclaims 'The horror! The horror!'. This Marlow interprets as 'a judgement upon the adventures of his soul on this earth'. Shortly afterwards the manager's boy announces in the now famous words: 'Mistah Kurtz – he dead' (p.100).

Marlow, too, nearly died. But, he says, 'I remained to dream the nightmare out to the end, and to show my loyalty to Kurtz once more' (p.100). He describes his unexciting contest with death. He has merely peeped over the edge of the precipice and now wonders whether, had he really died, he would have been able to utter as eloquent a cry as Kurtz. This, to him, is 'an affirmation, a moral victory' (p.101) dearly paid for. When Marlow returned to the 'sepulchral city' (Brussels) he could hardly bear the complacency of its inhabitants. He now realises, however, that his impressions were subjective, that after his experience in the jungle he was not in a normal state of mind and that his 'imagination . . . wanted soothing' (p.102). He receives the visit of several people who have known

Kurtz and who each emphasise a different aspect of his personality. The complete picture this creates gives indeed the impression that Kurtz was a 'universal genius' (p.103). To each visitor, except the threatening official, Marlow gives some of Kurtz's writings.

Finally, Marlow is stimulated to visit Kurtz's Intended after looking at her picture and noticing 'the delicate shade of truthfulness upon her features' (p.104). As he enters the house Marlow has a vision of Kurtz opening his mouth voraciously and feels as if the wilderness were entering with him. When the girl appears in the room it is getting darker and all the light seems to gather on her pure brow. Marlow is aware of the depth of her sorrow; he realises she is not likely to be the plaything of time, and he suddenly sees her and Kurtz together. In the ensuing conversation she questions Marlow eagerly about Kurtz, or rather she asks him questions and suggests answers to them herself, anxious to hear Marlow confirm that she knew and understood Kurtz best, loved him best, and that Kurtz was a great and noble man. All this time the darkness increases in the room and contrasts with the light on her head. Marlow does not contradict the Intended; he tells her what she wants to hear in spite of his anger and despair, of which she is utterly unaware. At one stage she puts out her arms in exactly the same way as Kurtz's black mistress. The she wants to know how Kurtz died and what his last words were. Marlow does not betray Kurtz. He lies and tells her that the last word Kurtz pronounced was her name. He has the impression that the house might collapse but, he says, 'the heavens do not fall for such a trifle' (p.111). His excuse for lying is that 'it would have been too dark – too dark altogether . . .' (p.111).

Marlow's tale is now ended. The first narrator once more comments on his Buddha-like position and closes the narrative by saying that 'the tranquil waterway . . . seemed to lead into the heart of an immense darkness' (p.111).

COMMENTARY: Marlow's renewed assertion that Kurtz is only a voice emphasises once more the nature of Kurtz's power, which lies wholly in the seductiveness of his eloquence; it also stresses his duality, the contrast between his idealism and the fake character of his achievement. Kurtz's insistence that one must always act for the right motives reveals the extent of his deception. It is worth comparing briefly Kurtz's last moment with the helmsman's. The latter gave Marlow a look 'like a distant kinship affirmed' (p.73), which suggests that the significance of his death may be relevant to all men. The 'supreme moment' of his death becomes in Kurtz's case 'that supreme moment of complete knowledge' (p.101). Kurtz can understand more clearly than the helmsman what is happening to him and that, too, is relevant to all men for 'his stare . . . was wide enough to embrace the whole universe, piercing enough to penetrate all the hearts that beat in the darkness'. Whatever the truth Kurtz has glimpsed, Marlow sees its perception as a 'moral victory'. In other words, he approves of Kurtz's achievement of consciousness; that is why he keeps thinking of him as a remarkable man and remains loyal to him.

When Marlow is back in Brussels the reader has the impression that he has escaped one kind of death but faces another, the death of the spirit. Indeed what strikes him is the blindness and 'folly' of the people he meets 'in the face of a danger [they are] unable to comprend' (p.102). Apart from the official who visits Marlow, the others' praise of Kurtz emphasises once more the greatness of which he seems to have been truly capable. But without realising it, the journalist puts his finger on the very danger of Kurtz's gifts when he says he ought to have gone into politics because he could electrify large meetings, could get himself to believe anything, and was an extremist. He thus puts into a nutshell all the reasons why Kurtz (and the European powers he clearly represents in this passage) could work up in himself and others a great enthusiasm for a cause which led him to the worst aberrations. This is brought home to the reader with greater force when Marlow visits the Intended and cannot dissociate his memory of the wilderness and of the voracious Kurtz from the idealism and the light that are so clearly impressed on her personality. Yet she too is self-deceived since she only wants from Marlow a confirmation of her faith in Kurtz. Marlow refuses to make her aware of the darkness in order to preserve her 'great and saving illusion' (p.108). This brings to mind two other statements by Marlow. One is to the effect that the 'idea' behind the colonial enterprise redeems it (p.10). The other is his assertion that women should stay in a 'beautiful world of their own' (p.69).

Notice also the contrast between the first narrator's early description of the Thames as 'a waterway leading to the utmost ends of the earth' (p.6), and its leading 'into the heart of an immense darkness' (p.111) at the end.

Part 3

Commentary

Ideological and historical background

Except for brief intervals when people reacted against imperialism, the history of Europe between the fifteenth and the twentieth centuries is strongly influenced by the expansionism of England, France, the Netherlands, Portugal, Spain, and later Germany and Belgium, as well as by their determination to build empires overseas. There have always been many arguments to excuse imperialism and, no doubt, there are many at the bottom of it. Economic historians have demonstrated that the conquest of unexploited areas of the world by Britain in the latter half of the nineteenth century was the only way out of the economic depression of the 1880s. Others have argued that at the end of the nineteenth century the economic case for annexing large areas of jungle or desert was not convincing, but no European power was prepared to stand by while its rivals extended their territories. Imperialism was also vindicated on moral grounds, particularly by missionaries. It was considered as a means of liberating peoples from tyrannical rule or of bringing them the blessings of the Christian religion and of a superior civilisation. Most people at the end of the nineteenth century were sincerely convinced of this, and even as enlightened a man as George Bernard Shaw (1856–1950) could argue that 'if the Chinese were incapable of establishing conditions in their own country which would promote peaceful commerce and civilised life, it was the duty of European powers to establish such conditions for them.'

The supporters of imperialism did not see it as a means of domination or exploitation. Lord Curzon (1859–1925), who was viceroy of India from 1898 to 1905, summed up their position clearly when he wrote: 'In empire, we have found not merely the key to glory and wealth, but the call to duty and the means of service to mankind'. Humanitarianism, a nineteenth-century movement concerned with human welfare, philanthropic activities and social reform, supported imperialism and sometimes exerted sufficient pressure to turn colonial concessions into enlightened centres, yet reacted against it when it turned out to be mere exploitation. By the end of the century, however, disillusionment prevailed as a result of the discrepancy between humanitarian ideals and the reality of colonial exploitation.

Nothing illustrates this more clearly than the colonisation of the Congo, which was part of the 'scramble for Africa'. In 1875 less than one-tenth of Africa had been turned into European colonies. By 1895 only one-tenth was not under European control. In the early 1880s several European powers, and the Belgian King Leopold II acting in his private capacity, were trying to control the Congo river basin peopled by independent tribal groups. The largest of them formed a kingdom called Congo and gave its name to the river. Leopold II became interested in Central Africa, at that time still a blank on the map, because he believed in his country's absolute need for a colony though he had the support of neither his government nor the Belgian people. For the purposes of exploration he founded the International Association for the Exploration and Civilisation of Africa, probably 'the International Society for the Suppression of Savage Customs' (p.71) in *Heart of Darkness*. In 1877 came the news that the British journalist and explorer Henry M. Stanley (1841–1904) had travelled across Africa over a period of three years. The British government were not interested in developing the Congo, and in 1878 Stanley entered the service of Leopold II. From 1879 to 1884 Stanley was in the Congo basin where he opened up the country, launched steamers on the upper river and established a chain of stations along the river up to Stanley Falls. At the end of the Berlin Conference (from November 1884 to February 1885), which had met to define a free-trade zone in Central Africa but actually dealt with the partition of Africa and the establishment of zones of influence, the Congo was recognised as an 'independent state' and became the Congo Free State under the personal sovereignty of King Leopold.

The King subsidised the State, sometimes with the help of Belgium. Financial problems were solved by the establishment of the *régime domanial,* by which all vacant land as well as its products – mainly ivory and rubber – were declared State property. It killed all private trade and soon made the State very prosperous. It was soon alleged that the compulsory collection of rubber led to bad treatment of the native population. Specific charges were made by the British Consul in Boma, Roger Casement (1864–1916), in a report published in 1904 by the British government. It led to a strong anti-Congolese campaign and the foundation of the Congo Reform Association. A commission of inquiry was sent to the Congo, which confirmed the existence of grave abuses. Although efforts were made to improve the situation, a complete change could only be imposed by transferring control of the State of Belgium. In spite of strong opposition by the socialists and some liberals, the Congo was officially annexed by Belgium on 15 November 1908.

The nature of the work

Much of Conrad's fiction is based on actual facts and personal experience. There is a sense in which *Heart of Darkness* is a 'Personal Record', for the autobiographical element is particularly strong in it. Conrad wrote about it: 'it is experience pushed a little (and only very little) beyond the actual facts of the case for the perfectly legitimate . . . purpose of bringing it home to the minds and bosoms of the readers.' The last part of the sentence suggests that it may have been Conrad's intention to make his readers aware of the situation that prevailed in the Congo when he travelled there. He does indeed make it clear that the colonisation of the Congo was, as he called it later, 'the vilest scramble for loot that ever disfigured the history of human conscience'. But he is not a reformer with a 'message' to put across, nor a historian who records facts objectively. He is essentially an artist who has transmuted his personal experience into a multi-levelled, multi-faceted narrative in which form is as important as content.

Heart of Darkness is the first of Conrad's novels or stories that achieves the complexity of a great work of art. Its implications are individual, social, political and metaphysical. One of its central themes, man's existential isolation ('we live, as we dream – alone') was to become a major theme in modern fiction. A corollary to it is the need for a personal code of behaviour and a capacity for moral discrimination as opposed to mere reliance on a public code, which often proves inadequate. The reader must be attentive to the small incidents through which Conrad distinguishes between an unreflecting and a genuinely felt moral attitude. The 'pilgrims', for example, are scandalised when Marlow throws his dead helmsman overboard or when he stays in the dining-room after Kurtz's death has been announced, because the public attitude to death must be one of mournful respect. But while Marlow is sincerely affected by both deaths, they are truly indifferent to the death of men around them, whether black or white. Similarly, a genuine concern for human beings informs Conrad's indictment of colonialism. Writing about his story 'the subject is of our time distinctly' when hardly anyone questioned the righteousness of colonial expansion, he was not merely referring to its topicality but indirectly drawing attention to the individual's share of responsibility for public events. His subject is also the individual consciousness of his hero, as it is of every modern novelist.

In his preface to *The Nigger of the Narcissus* Conrad defines the purpose of art as 'a single-minded attempt to render the highest kind of justice to the visible universe, by bringing to light the truth, manifold and one, underlying its every aspect.' He insists several times on the need to convey the 'very truth' or essence of the fragment of life the artist chooses to deal with. We may therefore ask ourselves *how* Conrad expresses the truth of the life experience he recreates. There are several comments in *Heart of Darkness* about the nature of Marlow's tale and, at a further remove, Conrad's. The first narrator calls Marlow's experience 'inconclusive' (p.10), and Marlow himself says that the significance of his meeting with Kurtz, though it 'seemed somehow to throw a kind of light . . . was . . . not very clear . . . no, not very clear' (p.11). This affirmation seems to hide a stratagem on Conrad's part. It is certainly true that at no point does Marlow draw a conclusion about his experience, unless his lie can be considered as one. Through the narrative he gropes for a meaning, and by doing so, indirectly invites the reader to take part in his search. That the meaning is not directly evident was acknowledged by Conrad himself in a letter to a friend: 'the idea is so wrapped up in secondary notions that you – even you! – may miss it'. He offers, however, a method of approach through the first narrator who says that to Marlow 'the meaning of an episode was not inside like a kernel but outside, enveloping the tale which brought it out only as a glow brings out a haze, in the likeness of one of these misty halos that sometimes are made visible by the spectral illumination of moonshine' (p.8). This is not an easy sentence because it does not qualify Marlow's story directly but through images: 'haze', 'misty halos', 'spectral illumination of moonshine'. They suggest a veiled diffuseness, by which Conrad may mean that the significance of the novel cannot be reduced to a simple clue that will 'disclose its inspiring secret'. The meaning is to be found everywhere; it must be looked for beyond the obvious, through the accretion of detail and the dense texture of the narrative.

The colonialist experience

Although Marlow's trip to the Congo lends itself to many interpretations, *Heart of Darkness* is (on one level at least) an inquiry into the nature of colonialism and a severe denunciation of it. At the same time it questions the value of white civilisation and the desirability of its transplantation to so-called primitive countries. As Marlow indirectly suggests by referring to the conquest of Britain by the Romans, colonialism has existed since the earliest times of human history. One of the merits of Conrad's novel is to present colonialism not as a political and economic venture only, but as a consequence of the individual's lust for power and possessiveness and even as an epitome of man's capacity for evil.

From the very beginning Conrad presents several approaches to colonialism. The anonymous narrator sees it only as a glorious adventure, at once an expression of England's greatness and a means of adding to it. He is not aware that by calling English conquerors 'hunters for gold or pursuers of fame' (p.7) he associates them with the Roman invaders who 'grabbed what they could for the sake of what was to be got' (p.10) and with all the characters in Marlow's tale who take part in the colonialist enterprise for selfish purposes. Nor does he realise that by pointing to the two symbols of that enterprise, 'the sword' and 'the torch' (p.7), he is actually referring to brutal force and to the negation of native culture by the so-called light of civilisation. His view of imperialism was naturally widespread at the end of the nineteenth century, but it is clear that, at this stage at least, he has not 'meditated over it'. Similarly, Marlow's aunt has an idealistic view of colonialism and is pleased with herself for helping to send Marlow to Africa as one of the 'Workers' and as an 'emissary of light'. She subscribes entirely to the view that the motive behind colonialism is to civilise the conquered peoples, 'weaning those ignorant millions from their horrid ways' (p.18). Her conception of the colonialist intention corresponds to that expressed by Rudyard Kipling in a poem called *The White Man's Burden,* which emphasises the ideals of duty and service ('To serve your captives' need') that inspired many who went to the colonies.

Although Marlow's mission is limited to the rescue of Kurtz, there is a sense in which his trip to the Congo is a recreation of the colonialist expedition, which enables him to understand its nature. We quoted in Part 2 his ambivalent definition of colonialism, asserting that what redeems it is the idea at the back of it. We may now wonder to what extent this dualistic view is substantiated by the narrative and by Marlow's confrontation with its reality. Already on his way out to Africa he notices that the only settlements seen from the coast are trading places with names out of some 'sordid farce' (p.19) while he thinks there is 'a touch of insanity' (p.20) about the man-of-war firing into the continent. Even at this early stage the colonial expedition strikes him as a 'merry dance of death and trade' (p.20) or as 'a weary pilgrimage amongst hints for nightmares' (p.21). Not until he comes to the 'grove of death', however, does he realise the full extent of the destructive process in which the whites are engaged in Africa. His suspicion that he will become acquainted with 'a flabby, pretending, weak-eyed devil of a rapacious and pitiless folly' (p.23) is immediately confirmed when he comes upon the dying negroes. What he ironically calls 'the work!' (p.24) is an irrational and meaningless violation of the land and its people. The transplantation of the trappings of white civilisation (the boiler and the railway-truck) and of a type of behaviour specific to it (the blasting on the hillside, the accountant's well-kept books, the 'law' which remains a mystery to the natives) seems to make no sense here. No effort is made by the colonialists to understand the alien population that they exploit as 'raw matter' (p.23). Marlow at least recognises the 'reality' and the 'otherness' of the native people, who remain an enigma to him but about whom he keeps asking himself questions; for example, he wonders at the restraint of the starving cannibals.

When Marlow sets out for the Central Station, he is made to see into the real motives that bring many a white man to Africa. His travelling companion, who keeps fainting in the heat, tells him that 'of course' he has come to make money (p.29). The manager is a 'common trader' (p.31) and his agents have turned ivory into a god. Their hatred of Kurtz as a successful collector of ivory points to the corrupting influence of their enterprise. As to the members of the Eldorado Exploring Expedition, their unashamed desire is 'to tear treasure out of the bowels of the land . . . with no more moral purpose at the back of it than there is in burglars breaking into a safe' (p.44).

Before Marlow actually meets him, Kurtz seems to be a very different type of colonialist since even his detractors acknowledge that he is an idealist and that he has come out 'equipped with moral ideas' (p.44). He remains an idealist to the very end, discoursing eloquently to Marlow on his death-bed. Yet he has become a ruthless exploiter, who is prepared to kill for a little ivory. Instead of turning his station into 'a beacon on the road towards better things', as he intended to, 'a centre . . . for humanising, improving, instructing' (p.47), he has given in to the 'fascination of the abomination' (p.9), as his participation in 'unspeakable rites' (p.71) and the human heads on poles around his house indicate. Conrad, of course, does not criticise primitive customs as such but the Europeans' return to them. Before meeting Kurtz, Marlow had described the colonialist experience as 'unreal' (pp.33 and 35) and called it a 'fantastic invasion' (pp.33 and 47). Gradually building up the personality of Kurtz for his listeners, he exposes the contradiction inherent in colonialism, the discrepancy between the Europeans' words, particularly their public utterances, and their actions. The contrast between Kurtz's 'burning noble words' and the criminal postscript to his report 'Exterminate all the brutes!' (p.72) is a stroke of genius, for this is what reveals the extent of Kurtz's self-deception and the failure of white civilisation to put its ideals into practice. More than that, it shows the perversion of those ideals. As one modern writer puts it, 'Does order breed extermination of others in the name of purity or virtue?'. White civilisation has been tested in Kurtz and found wanting.

Why then does Marlow say that the 'idea' at the back of colonialism redeems it? Admittedly, after drawing attention to the white man's limitations and exposing his sense of superiority as sham, he calls it an 'illusion' (p.108) but a 'great and saving' illusion to which he bows his head as if it were an idol or a fetish. Why does he lie to Kurtz's Intended, not only about Kurtz himself but about the real character of the colonialist experience? Like much in *Heart of Darkness*, Marlow's lie lends itself to many interpretations. To suggest that he lied out of compassion for the Intended is inadequate, for he does not lie merely to protect her from knowledge. The illusion 'redeems' the rest of the civilised world as well. Marlow's excuse, 'It would have been too dark – too dark altogether' (p.111), shows that his is a protective lie, and we must remember that earlier in his tale he said 'We must help [women] to stay in that beautiful world of their own, *lest ours gets worse*' (p.69, italics mine). The 'illusion' is thus, as Jacques Berthoud points out (*Joseph Conrad, the Major Phase*, 1978, p.63), a positive one, for it offers an alternative to mere corruption or the ignorance of it and at least helps men like Marlow to live up to their ideals of efficiency and restraint.

There is, however, another possible interpretation of the lie. Marlow's attitude towards the Africans is not utterly devoid of paternalism. But, on the whole, he systematically undermines the role of white civilisation, exposing its shortcomings and deceptions; while at the same time, by calling Africa and its people an 'enigma', he recognises that they have a specific character which the white man should try to understand. This was revolutionary enough in Conrad's time and ran counter to all ingrained prejudices. Possibly Conrad felt that he could go no further, and he may have made a concession to his contemporaries by allowing Marlow to insist on the value of the saving ideal even if it was illusory and at the cost of a lie.

Several critics have asserted that in *Heart of Darkness* Conrad criticised Belgian colonialism only, but approved of the work done by the British in their colonies. Their argument, apart from what is known of Conrad's admiration for the English, is that when Marlow looks at a map of the world in the company's office, he comments: 'There was a vast amount of red – good to see at any time, because one knows that some real work is done in there' (p.14). There is no denying the atrocious conditions of Belgian colonisation nor their impact on Conrad, and he may well have had in mind the kind of distinction put forward by the defenders of British imperialism. But this is not how the novel reads nowadays, and to suggest that Conrad condemned one kind of colonialism and admired another is to restrict its significance. Marlow's comment is, indeed, belied by the text. The juxtaposition of the nameless narrator's praise of the greatness of British conquerors with Marlow's description of Roman colonialism throws an ironic light on British achievement. Marlow's definition of colonialism (p.10) is general and applies to all such enterprises. Kurtz has been educated partly in England and his mother was half-English. 'All Europe', says

Marlow, 'contributed to the making of Kurtz' (p.71), and his self-deception clearly applies to all European imperialism. It is not impossible that in Marlow's reflection Conrad was playing up to his audience.

Journey into the self

Heart of Darkness does not deal exclusively with colonialism. It also recreates a voyage of self-discovery and is often described as a story of initiation or, as Albert Guerard puts it, a 'night journey'. How does Conrad reconcile the two aspects of Marlow's experience, that is, his confrontation with the reality of colonialism and an introspective voyage leading to spiritual change? No doubt one of the story's greatest achievements is that the actual voyage should, through Conrad's symbolic language, evoke a journey into the self. But it is also essential to realise that Conrad does not present two separate issues, a public one (colonialism) and a private one (knowledge of the self). The two are indissociable, and Marlow's story clearly implies that the kind of world men make for themselves (and for others) largely results from the character of individual behaviour. For example, Kurtz's will-to-power (and that of men like him) lies at the core of colonialism, which is also what the manager, his 'faithless pilgrims', and the members of the El Dorado Expedition make it. Like these men, Marlow has been cut off from his original background and faces an alien environment. One essential difference between them and Marlow lies in his aware-ness that his moral being is subjected to a trial, and in his attempt to understand the significance of his experience.

We must remember that Marlow, not Kurtz, is the main character. In fact, Kurtz's appearance in the story is comparatively brief, and even then Marlow deals as much with his own reactions to Kurtz as with Kurtz himself. At the beginning of his tale Marlow refers to their meeting as 'the culminating point of my experience. It seemed some-how to throw a kind of light on everything about me – and into my thoughts' (p.11). When he repairs the steamboat at the Central Station and meditates on the effect of work, he says 'I like what is in the work, – the chance to find yourself. Your own reality . . . what no other man can know' (p.41). And when he returns to Brussels, he is irritated by the complacency of the people he meets in the street, feeling that 'they could not possibly know the things [he] knew' (p.102).

Marlow's trip from Europe to the Outer, then to the Central, Station already tests his capacity to discriminate between good and evil since he witnesses actions that elicit a moral judgement from him, such as the futile firing of a man-of-war into the African continent, and what amounts to genocide at the grove of death. His detailed account of what he sees there shows his compassion, which contrasts with the accountant's indifference and fits of hatred. There also he hears of Kurtz for the first time and from then on becomes gradually obsessed with a desire to meet him.

When they finally leave for the Inner Station, Marlow says 'For me it [the boat] crawled towards Kurtz – exclusively' (p.50). Immediately afterwards he declares 'We penetrated deeper and deeper into the heart of darkness' (p.50). This conjunction of Kurtz with the heart of darkness sums up the ultimate purpose of Marlow's exploration. In the course of his journey up-river the narrative acquires an increasingly symbolical meaning, and the landscape becomes a psychological as much as a physical reality. This is conveyed by Marlow's insistence that the 'earth seemed unearthly' (p.51) and that his experience has a dream-like quality, as well as by a growing impression that they lose the support of the material world. 'We were cut off from the comprehension of our surroundings' (p.51), says Marlow, and further 'The rest of the world was nowhere, as far as our eyes and ears were concerned. Just nowhere' (p.57). They are by then surrounded by a thick fog which makes them deaf and blind (p.56), and this obliteration of the senses symbolically anticipates the moral situation in which Kurtz has placed himself at the Inner Station (named symbolically too). Indeed, Marlow calls him an 'initiated wraith from the back of Nowhere' (p.71). When he actually fights with him, he explains that Kurtz 'had kicked himself loose of the earth. . . . He was alone, and I before him did not know whether I stood on the ground or floated in the air' (p.95).

We saw that as Marlow penetrates further into the unknown, his capacity for self-control and 'inborn strength' are tested. His real trial, however, only takes place when he feels he has been 'transported into some lightless region of subtle horrors' (p.83) which Kurtz seems to inhabit. Kurtz is repeatedly described as a shadow, and when Marlow tries to convey the essence of his experience, he declares 'I am trying to account to myself for – for – Mr Kurtz – for the shade of Mr Kurtz' (p.71). Though Kurtz exists as a character in his own right, there is a sense in which he is also Marlow's shadow or 'double'. By declaring that Kurtz is 'a remarkable man' (p.89) Marlow was lumped together with him, and this identification with the 'nightmare of [his] choice' (p.92) leads to his confrontation with him. It accounts for the 'moral shock' Marlow receives when he realises that Kurtz has left the steamboat to join the natives; and for his statement 'I was anxious to deal with this shadow by myself alone – and to this day I don't know why I was so jealous of sharing with any one the peculiar blackness of that experience' (pp.92–3). When Marlow states 'I confounded the beat of the drum with the beating of my heart' (p.93), he shows that, like

Kurtz, he has reached the heart of darkness, 'the farthest point of navigation' (p.11). It is no longer with the wilderness outside that Marlow fights, but rather with its effect on Kurtz and the spell it cast over him. 'If anybody ever struggled with a soul', he says, 'I am the man' (p.95). That Marlow's involvement with Kurtz amounts to a plunge into the depths of the self is confirmed when he explains that Kurtz's soul had looked within itself, and . . . gone mad. I had . . . to go through the ordeal of looking into it myself' (p.95). Whatever Marlow's arguments, he not only succeeds in bringing Kurtz back to the boat, but remains sufficiently detached to judge with precision the extent of his self-deception, the fact that Kurtz still hides 'in the magnificent folds of eloquence the barren darkness of his heart' (p.98).

Marlow himself does not achieve complete self-knowledge. This, he says, 'comes too late' (p.100) at the moment of death. But he comes as near to it as is possible when he witnesses Kurtz's confrontation with death and, after the 'veil ha[s] been rent' (p.99), hears him exclaim 'The horror! The horror!' (p.100). That is why he says 'It is *his* extremity that I seem to have lived through' (p.101, italics mine). He interprets this exclamation as 'a judgement upon the adventures of his soul on earth' (p.100). He also asserts that 'it had candour, it had conviction . . . it had the appalling face of a glimpsed truth' (p.101). Thus when he steps 'over the threshold of the invisible' (p.101), Kurtz at last achieves awareness of what he is. Hence Marlow's affirmation that his cry is 'a moral victory' (p.101). He also discovers some general truth about mankind since 'his stare . . . was wide enough to embrace the whole universe, piercing enough to penetrate all the hearts that beat in the darkness' (p.101). This moment of vision has been fore-shadowed by Kurtz's willingness to be taken back to the boat without making a row. As to Marlow, who also struggled with death but only 'peeped over the edge' (p.101), he found that, were he really to die, he would have nothing to say. His experience, however, seems to have shattered all his former assumptions about man. Already in the short story *An Outpost of Progress* Conrad had stated that 'the contact with pure unmitigated savagery . . . excites the imagination' and shown in what way it is challenged and tried. After his return from the Congo Marlow comments: 'it was my imagination that wanted soothing' (p.102). This, if need be, is another confirmation of the doctor's assertion that 'the changes take place inside' (p.17).

A glimpsed truth

Marlow's first words in *Youth* are 'You fellows know there are those voyages that seem ordered for the illustration of life, that might stand for a symbol of existence'. *Heart of Darkness* deals with one such voyage and has been called a 'poetic meditation on human existence'. The reader cannot fail to be struck by Marlow's repeated self-questioning about the behaviour of men, whether black or white, as well as about man's position in the universe and the meaning of life. These questions arise as a result of Marlow's confrontation with 'the mystery of an unknown earth' (p.7); they are his reaction to a typically Conradian situation, that of the hero who is cut off from family, friends, habitual social environment, and tested in a crisis gone through in 'isolation' (p.19). One of his first discoveries as he travels away from his familiar surroundings is an alteration of what can be termed 'real', and a sense of the relativity of reality. On the African coast only the surf and the paddling negroes give him a sense of 'reality' (p.19), of something 'natural and true' (p.20). When he arrives at the Central Station, the whites and their dealings seem to him increasingly 'unreal' (pp.33 and 35) while, by contrast, he is impressed by the wilderness as 'something great and invincible' (p.33), by the mystery of the land and 'the amazing reality of its concealed life' (p.37). Marlow opposes two different views of reality. One of them is linked with the value of work as an instrument of self-discovery: 'I like what is in the work – the chance to find yourself. Your own reality' (p.41). This is largely synonymous with what he calls elsewhere 'inborn strength' and 'deliberate belief' (p.52) and it also manifests itself in his capacity for restraint. These qualities are not the white man's privilege, as Marlow himself insists when he presents the cannibals as 'fine fellows . . . men one could work with' (pp.49–50), who also show 'restraint' and 'inborn strength' (p.60).

The other reality Marlow presents is embodied in the landscape. When he refers to 'the overwhelming realities of this strange world of plants, and water and silence' and adds 'It was the stillness of an implacable force brooding over an inscrutable intention' (p.48), he seems to discern in the African landscape an indefinable presence, at once fascinating and threatening, 'an appeal or . . . a menace'. 'What was in there?' (p.38) he asks. No final or clear answer is given to this question, and Marlow asserts that 'The inner truth is hidden – luckily, luckily' (p.49). True, he had just described the appeal of the manager's uncle 'to the hidden evil' in the land. Does this mean, as is often suggested, that the reality at the heart of primitive nature is positively malignant? It seems rather that Marlow (or Conrad through him) presents untamed nature as the seat of a force that man is too small to comprehend, and uses it as a reflector of that unknown part of man's psyche which is itself the seat of contradictory impulses such as Kurtz illustrates (see pp.98 and 101). This may be part of Kurtz's 'glimpsed truth' (p.101) and explains the 'commingling of desire and hate' (p.101) in his final cry. As Marlow says, 'life is a greater riddle than some of us think it to be' (p.101). What is certain is that the opposition between the reality of work, the capacity for achievement, and that of the living wilderness is at the centre of his vision of the world.

Even before formulating this antithesis of truth in the universe and man's 'own true stuff' (p.52), Marlow asks another fundamental question: 'What were we who had strayed in here?' (p.38). This is answered piecemeal in the course of the narrative. We saw in Part 2 that, when confronted with a great and mysterious nature, man seems very small. While praising the saving virtue of efficiency, Marlow describes his work as 'monkey tricks' on a tight-rope (p.49). He further compares his progress on the river to that of a 'blindfolded man set to drive a van over a bad road' (p.49). These can be read as images for man's progress and performances in life. They suggest that, however seriously he takes himself, man is like an animal performing well but dangerously and for no clear purpose in a universe which he does not comprehend. It is as if the gods had wanted to make game of him, and it throws an ironic light on the white man's claim to infallibility and his view of himself as a 'supernatural being' (p.72). In addition, Marlow states that what keeps the white man on the right path is the butcher, who saves him from the necessity of being a cannibal, and the policeman; that is, the institutions which civilised society sets up to ensure order. Without the support and check of these institutions man yields to his 'forgotten and brutal instincts' or to his 'monstrous passions' (pp.94–5), as Kurtz does, or like Decoud in *Nostromo*, he gives in to despair and commits suicide.

It seems then that for Marlow (and Conrad) civilisation is a varnish which wears off as soons as man is cut off from the conditions that created it. Marlow's trip is also a return 'to the earliest beginnings of the world' (p.48) into 'the night of first ages' (p.51). We can deduce from this that he views primitive man as the ancestor of so-called civilised man, an opinion confirmed by his response to the wilderness as to the past of man (pp.51–2). The point Marlow emphasises, however, is his awareness of kinship with the natives: 'what thrilled you was just the thought of their humanity – like yours' (p.51). It is not merely his wish to go ashore 'for a howl and a dance' (p.52) that makes him affirm their common humanity, but the inarticulate (though eloquent) look of his helmsman as he dies (p.73).

One conclusion we can draw from these comments is that Conrad considerably widens the scope of fiction by presenting man not in society, as is usually the case in the novel, but in a grandiose nature, giving Marlow's reflections a universal dimension. His presentation of a reality other than man's individual and social props was also new at the time. The ease with which civilised man can discard the virtues that make for self-control and achievement in a situation of prolonged stress seems to have been the cause of Conrad's pessimism, even despair. These throw another light on Marlow's lie, which can also be explained as a refusal to question further the values of white civilisation. Like Winnie Verloc in *The Secret Agent*, Conrad seems to have been of opinion that 'things do not stand much looking into'.

The main characters

Apart from Kurtz, Marlow, and his predecessor, Fresleven, none of the other characters are given a name. They are called after their function, which suggests that they are types rather than strongly individualised figures, and emphasises the symbolical meaning of Marlow's tale.

Marlow

In his introduction to *Youth*, the story in which Marlow appears for the first time as second, and chief, narrator, Conrad says of him: 'He haunts my hours of solitude, when, in silence, we lay our heads together in great comfort and harmony'. This might lead us to suppose that Marlow is Conrad's *alter ego* and a mere mouthpiece for him. It is not quite so, however. By using Marlow as an intermediary between himself and the other characters, Conrad achieves a detachment which it might have been more difficult for him to maintain had he dealt straightforwardly with autobiographical material. As it is, Marlow is at once involved in the story, since his progress in understanding is its main subject, and a commentator who, in spite of his often non-committal tone, subtly directs the reader's response to his tale. We feel he is a trustworthy narrator, yet we judge him as a fallible human being with a normal capacity for good and evil and liable to make the same errors as those he denounces in others.

We saw above that the significance of the novel grows out of Marlow's expedition and his return as a changed man. In one way at least he is an exceptional man: 'The worst that could be said of him was that he did not represent his class. He was a seaman, but he was a wanderer, too, while most seamen lead, if one may so express it, a sedentary life. Their minds are of the stay-at-home order' (p.8). This suggests that, unlike other sailors, Marlow has an active imaginary life and is a traveller in the 'country of the mind'. His comments on the 'pilgrims' and the way in which he dissociates himself from them shows that he has already progressed in self-knowledge. The same can be said of his encounters with the harlequin and Kurtz, which force him to define his own position. What differentiates him most from the other characters is his capacity for moral discrimination.

Marlow himself offers a good example of the complexity of human behaviour and of the impossibility for man to remain untainted by evil. He has a little in common with all the other characters. Ironically, like the ancient colonists who had 'good friends in Rome' (p.9), like the manager and Kurtz, he obtains his post through recommendation, and is involved even against his will in a struggle for power, as Kurtz's comment 'I am glad' (p.86) shows. Like Kurtz, he is represented 'as an exceptional and gifted creature' (p.17) and an 'emissary of light' (p.18). He is aware, however, that this makes him an 'impostor' (p.18), which suggests that one cannot serve colonialism without being corrupted by it. He too resembles 'an idol' (p.6) and is several times compared to a Buddha either 'preaching in European clothes' (p.10), which naturally recalls Kurtz, or – at the end of the tale – 'meditating' (p.111), which may convey the wisdom he has attained. Like Kurtz (p.46), he prefers at one stage to turn to the wilderness (p.89) rather than face the manager's particular evil. He is not without his own contradictions as, for instance, when he declares 'Mr Kurtz was no idol of mine' (p.84) yet shortly afterwards admits that he had 'to invoke him – himself – his own exalted and incredible degradation' (p.95) as if Kurtz were some kind of evil god that had to be placated. His most obvious contradiction is when he says that he detests and can't bear a lie (p.38) yet lies first to the brickmaker, and is aware of being a 'pretence' (p.39) too – then, more significantly, lies to Kurtz's Intended. Tearing off the postscript from Kurtz's report is also a kind of lie.

These contradictions indicate that Conrad creates human beings as they are, not as they ought to be; also, that each situation demands a new choice and not a blind adherence to a code. Certainly, Marlow is a balanced and positive character, equally distrustful of self-righteousness and claims to superiority. He is sensitive and humane, a man who knows his own mind and rejects both the white man's exploitation of the natives and his surrender to sheer primitiveness. Above all, Marlow pleads for authenticity (one's 'own true stuff') and this is linked with his moral awareness. His main role in the narrative is, to use Conrad's own words in his preface to *The Nigger of the Narcissus*, to make us '*see*', and indeed the reader sometimes sees more than Marlow himself – which prevents him, for example, from sharing Marlow's admiration for the accountant. Marlow's instrument, like Kurtz's, is his eloquence. Just as he keeps referring to Kurtz as 'little more than a voice' (pp.69 and 86), so the first narrator says of him that he was 'no more . . . than a voice' (p.39). Like Marlow, the reader must learn to discriminate between a gift which is used to exalt yet deceive (as Kurtz does) and a gift which is used to give pleasure and edify.

Kurtz

Kurtz may be said to represent the best and the worst of which the white man is capable. His portrait is built up long before he actually appears. Everyone is full of him. The accountant at the Outer Station calls him 'a very remarkable person', though, when further questioned, he only adds that Kurtz 'sends in as much ivory as all the others put together' (p.27). At the Central Station the brickmaker calls him (with a mixture of hate and envy) 'a special being' and 'an emissary of pity, and science, and progress, and devil knows what else' (p.36). He belongs to the 'gang of virtue' and, before he meets him, Marlow admires his humanitarianism and romantic idealism, though he is curious to find out how Kurtz's 'moral ideas' (p.44) will stand the test of experience. The first real glimpse he has of Kurtz is provided by an image to which he (and the reader) responds imaginatively, that of Kurtz turning his back 'on the headquarters . . . on thoughts of home . . . setting his face towards the depths of the wilderness' (p.46). This image sums up what has happened to Kurtz. But it is only when Marlow sees the shrunken heads on poles that his former image of Kurtz suddenly collapses.

Kurtz's idealism and desire to bring the light of white civilisation to Africa are inseparable from his inordinate pride and will-to-power. This applies to him both as an individual and as an agent of Europe, which takes its own superiority for granted. His many gifts as a musician, a painter, a journalist, and a politician make him truly representative of a highly sophisticated culture. He is an arch-egoist and keeps talking to Marlow of '*my* Intended, *my* ivory, *my* station, *my* river' (p.70, italics mine. See also p.98). Conrad once wrote that 'A man haunted by a fixed idea is insane. He is dangerous even if that idea is the idea of justice'. He alludes here to the perversion of idealism that inevitably follows the uncontrolled wish to achieve one's ends. Marlow is appalled to discover human heads on the fence surrounding Kurtz's station, to hear that he took part in 'unspeakable rites' (p.71) and that he was prepared to kill the harlequin, who has saved his life, for a little ivory. He attributes the transformation of virtue into vice in Kurtz to his lack of 'restraint' and adds 'there was something wanting in him – some small matter which, when the pressing need arose, could not be found under his magnificent eloquence' (p.83). The suggestion here is that Kurtz's love of words is not matched by a moral sense which could save him in moments of crisis; it has become a mere façade hiding a hollowness which, as pointed out in Part 2 of these Notes, is different from the manager's. Hence the contradiction in his report between the expression of 'every altruistic sentiment' and 'Exterminate all the brutes!' (p.72). Hence also Marlow's own description of Kurtz's eloquence in ambivalent terms (p.68) and his contradictory reaction to it, saying in one place 'It made me tingle with enthusiasm' (p.72) but calling the memory of it 'one immense jabber . . . without any kind of sense' (p.69).

Kurtz remains a divided being to the last. He ordered the attack to be launched on the whites, but when they reach the station he lets them take him away and prevents the tribesmen from launching another attack. Once on the boat he leaves it to join the tribesmen; but when Marlow comes for him, he does not make the row that might lead to a massacre of the whites. Until just before dying he is a self-deceived idealist, yet seems to be engaged in a personal contest with the wilderness: 'Oh, but I will wring your heart yet!' he exclaims. And Marlow insists that up to the moment of death he struggled with himself (pp.95 and 98). By wanting to become a god and giving up all restraint he has actually become a devil, a slave to the wilderness (in his heart and in the forest) which he intended to subdue. In Kurtz Conrad points to the danger of spiritual pride, of presuming that man can measure himself against forces he cannot even gauge.

What is to be our final assessment of Kurtz? Marlow says that 'Whatever he was, he was not common' (p.72). He repeats several times that Kurtz is a remarkable man (pp.89, 101 and 107) because of his extraordinary gifts, because he is at least involved in a spiritual struggle, which the manager and his pilgrims ignore or despise, and because his final cry shows that he eventually understands the nature of his perversion. He also says, however, that he was not 'worth the life we lost in getting to him' (p.73). If we put together all Marlow's comments about Kurtz, we will see that the image we get remains full of contradictions, and this illustrates the good and the evil of which he, like any man, is capable. It has been suggested that Kurtz is a tragic hero – someone who aspires to a greatness and fulfilment which his human condition prevents him from attaining. But this is to reduce his responsibility for his own degradation and for the total failure of his humanitarian ideals.

The accountant

The accountant is the first white man Marlow meets when he reaches the Congo. His impeccable outfit offers such a contrast to the dying natives at the grove of death that Marlow at first takes him for a 'miracle' (p.25), although by calling him 'a hairdresser's dummy' (p.26), he seems to present an automaton rather than a man. The accountant presents Marlow with one kind of aberration in the so-called civilising enterprise: futile and heartless efficiency. Marlow expresses admiration for what he has achieved: with great difficulty he has taught a native woman to clean and starch his collars and shirt-fronts, and his books are in 'apple-pie order' (p.26). There seems to be no irony in Marlow's admiration, which fits in with his respect for efficient work. Conrad, however, makes sure we do not share it by contrasting ironically the accountant's immaculate clothing with the muddle around him, and above all by showing in what way he illustrates the 'philanthropic pretence'. His complete blindness to the horrors of the grove of death when he comes out 'to get a breath of fresh air' (p.26) and his indifference to, even impatience with, the sufferings of the dying agent, reveal his egoism and insensitiveness. In his vanity and hatred of the natives he anticipates Kurtz, whom he so much admires. He is self-controlled and competent only at the cost of his dehumanisation.

The manager and his 'faithless pilgrims'

The manager is Marlow's other 'choice of nightmares' (p.89), whose cynicism contrasts with Kurtz's self-deceptive idealism. Unlike Kurtz, he is a commonplace man with 'no genius . . . no learning, and no intelligence' (p.31), who can only keep the routine going but 'originate[s] nothing'. His ineptitude is an ironic comment on the civilisers' claim to intellectual and technological superiority. He has reached his position only because he is never ill. Marlow explains that his endurance is due to his inner emptiness: 'Perhaps there was nothing within him' (p.31). His hollowness is positively evil, the expression of his amorality. Marlow's feeling that the manager is capable of anything inspires him with uneasiness. His impression is confirmed when the manager countenances his uncle's assertion that 'Anything – anything can be done in this country' (p.46). He has not waited for his uncle's cynical comment, 'The climate may do away with this difficulty [Kurtz] for you' (p.45), to make sure that it does. He has probably sunk the steamer intentionally just before Marlow's arrival and he sees to it that Marlow does not get the rivets to repair it, thus further delaying the rescue of Kurtz. The manager, also, would kill the harlequin if he found him too troublesome.

With those of his kind the manager cynically denies all human values, as when he refers to the 'pestiferous absurdity' of Kurtz's talk (p.47). He does not criticise Kurtz for getting ivory by exploiting the natives and calls his method 'unsound' (p.89) out of sheer envy. However deluded Kurtz may be, one can at least believe in his sincerity. The manager is not only an intriguer (see his conversation with his uncle) but a hypocrite. He pretends to be anxious about Kurtz's illness (p.32). Though the rescue of Kurtz is a pretence since he was left alone for so long, the manager wants to preserve appearances, the only 'restraint' of which he is capable. His comment to Marlow 'I authorise you to take all the risks' when he knows Marlow must refuse, contradicts his later statement 'Cautiously, cautiously – that's my principle' (p.89). He can say anything because he has no inner conviction, and his mean-spirited comments on Kurtz create 'an atmosphere so vile' (p.89) on the boat that Marlow turns for relief to the wilderness.

The absence of any real sense of responsibility in the manager is reflected in the behaviour of his agents, whom Marlow ironically calls 'faithless' and 'bewitched' pilgrims. Indeed, their behaviour is a parody of the purposefulness that ought to inspire their mission. With long staves in their hands they '[stroll] aimlessly about in the sunshine' (p.33), and they revere ivory like an idol: 'You would think they were praying to it' (p.33). They serve, in fact, the 'flabby, pretending, weak-eyed devil of a rapacious and pitiless folly' (p.23) which presides over the colonialist enterprise. They too are 'hollow men' behaving with cowardice and madness, as when they fire blindly into the bush when they reach the Inner Station. These men are responsible for 'the great demoralisation of the land' (p.26). No wonder Marlow sees their station and everything about them as 'unreal' (p.33).

The members of the Eldorado Exploring Expedition can be compared to the pilgrims although they are, if possible, even worse. 'Their talk . . . was the talk of sordid buccaneers: it was reckless without hardihood, greedy without audacity, and cruel without courage' (p.43). The manager's uncle is a cynic without scruples who helps his nephew in his intrigues and bluntly hopes that the jungle will kill Kurtz.

The brickmaker

He is one of the 'pilgrims' but stands out among them as a particularly striking example of their uselessness. He is supposed to make bricks but has been at the station for more than a year just waiting for the necessary material, 'backbiting and intriguing' (p.35) like his fellow agents, who think he is 'the manager's spy upon them' (p.34). He seems to be in league with his superior and to receive special treatment. There is in his hut a silver-mounted dressing case and a whole candle, while no-one else is entitled to them; an empty champagne bottle; and some African trophies, which suggests that he has already ransacked the land for pieces of African art. He is an aristocrat but vulgar in his purposes and the means used to reach them. He wants to become assistant-manager not through merit but by intrigue, and shamelessly pumps Marlow about his acquaintances in Brussels, feeling threatened by him as much as by Kurtz.

The brickmaker could be taken as a parody of Kurtz. He pays lip-service to Kurtz's ideals and *declaims*, that is, he repeats in a theatrical and rhetorical manner the eloquent words of idealists without meaning them at all. When a fire breaks out at night and creates an inferno-like background enhanced by the groans of a beaten negro, the brick-maker appears to Marlow as a 'papier-maché Mephistopheles', which fits in with the farcical pretensions of the cause he supposedly serves. With his 'forked little beard and a hooked nose' he has the appearance of one, too. Kurtz, who has 'taken a high seat amongst the devils of the land' (p.70), must at least be taken seriously. In the presence of this other 'hollow man' Marlow is the more impressed by the powerful reality of the jungle: 'All this was great, expectant, mute, while the man jabbered about himself' (p.38).

The harlequin

The harlequin is Marlow's most enigmatic encounter in the jungle. His first perception of the kind of man the harlequin may be is given him through the book he has left behind, *An Inquiry into some Points of Seamanship*. In its 'honest concern for the right way of going to work' (p.54) Marlow detects a foil to the surrounding wilderness. The harlequin has indeed survived without apparently being touched by it. Like Marlow, he is efficient, wholly self-reliant, and has carefully planned his escape from the Inner Station. He is, however, an ambiguous character. Smiles and frowns, sunshine and shadow alternate on his face. His youth seems to be a virtue in itself and the secret of his capacity for survival:

> The glamour of youth enveloped his parti-coloured rags, his destitu-tion, his loneliness, the essential desolation of his futile wander-ings . . . there he was gallantly, thoughtlessly alive, to all appearances indestructible solely by the virtue of his few years and of his un-reflecting audacity. (p.78)

Like Marlow, the harlequin is fascinated by Kurtz. But his devotion to him is blind and morally naive: 'He had not meditated over it . . . and he accepted it with a sort of eager fatalism' (p.79). His uneasiness while talking to Marlow about Kurtz's exploits shows that he senses Kurtz's perversity but cannot judge it. When piqued by Marlow's teasing, he can only say vaguely 'He made me see things – things' (p.79), which amounts to saying that he could see nothing, and is a sign of his immaturity. He idolises Kurtz in the same way as the natives and, in Marlow's words, 'crawled as much as the veriest savage of them all' (p.84). Just as he keeps saying about the natives 'They are simple people' (pp.76 and 90), he says about himself 'I am a simple man' (pp.84 and 90).

The harlequin seems to have much in common with the fool or trickster who appears in all literary traditions, whether Renaissance English drama, Italian *commedia dell'arte*, American-Indian or African folk-tales. As his parti-coloured rags suggest, he is a man without a fixed identity and therefore adaptable, who eludes the tyrannies of the established order (such as the manager and his acolytes represent) thanks to his cunning and occasional humour. In his pre-social and fluid state he seems to embody all possibilities of human development.

The natives

Marlow's approach to the natives reflects both Conrad's revolutionary outlook and the fact that it was partly overshadowed by the conditions and prejudices of the period in which he wrote. The first example of this duality occurs when Marlow comments on the negroes he sees along the African coast: 'they had faces like grotesque masks . . . but they had bone, muscle, a wild vitality, an intense energy of movement, that was as natural and true as the surf along their coast' (p.20). The reference to 'grotesque masks' is as pejorative nowadays as Marlow's portrait of the fireman as 'a dog in a parody of breeches and a feather hat, walking on his hind-legs' (p.52), though no more so than comparing white men to monkeys on a tight-rope. Marlow's use of the word 'nigger', generally accepted at the end of the nineteenth century, also sounds offensive today. On the whole, however, Marlow greatly admires the natives who still fit into their environment and have preserved their cultural identity, like Kurtz's black mistress, but he comments disparagingly on those who have become detribalised, the 'reclaimed' (p.23) who imitate the white man, like the leader of the chained slave gang at the grove of death.

Marlow does not make the mistake of confusing all Africans as white people often do even now. He discriminates between the tribes who live and work in their country of origin, like the cannibals, and the Africans who have been brought in from the coast and (like the white man) are 'lost in uncongenial surroundings, fed on unfamiliar food' (p.24), and therefore sicken and become inefficient. He is indignant at the way 'men – men, I tell you' (p.23) are being treated. The most eloquent expression of Marlow's imaginative response to Africa and its peoples is to be found in his admiration for the cannibals' self-possession when they are in danger and for their restraint when they are hungry. His realisation that their intended cannibalism calls for a reaction other than mere prejudice shows his understanding of other cultures. Marlow's appreciation of the natives, however, seems to be denied later by his lie to Kurtz's Intended.

The helmsman

Like the fireman, he is a detribalised African, an 'improved specimen' (p.52), says Marlow ironically, who has come from the coast and been trained by Fresleven. He has thus been cut off from his own community and has lost the dignity and the 'inborn strength' characteristic of the inland natives. As a result he has become 'unstable', foolishly proud one moment and abjectly frightened the next. When the steamboat is attacked by Kurtz's followers, he loses his self-control completely and becomes like 'a tree [swayed] by the wind' (pp.64 and 73). His frantic behaviour contrasts with the 'fierce and steady' expression of their assailants. He is responsible for his own death since he was wounded by a spear after opening the shutter of the pilot-house. His inquiring glance as he dies seems to express his confusion and disorientation, though the reality he has denied appears to take over again as his glance acquires a 'sombre, brooding, and menacing expression' (p.67). The scene of his death anticipates the other confrontation between black and white values that plays itself out when Kurtz dies. Marlow deplores that, like Kurtz, 'He had no restraint, no restraint' (p.73) and laments his death because of the subtle bond created between them by their work together.

Kurtz's native mistress

Kurtz's African mistress is a kind of black muse, the living spirit of primitive Africa and of its 'fecund and mysterious life' (p.87). Marlow first sees her as 'a wild and gorgeous apparition' (p.87). He presents her in the same ambivalent terms as he does the jungle: 'She was savage and superb, wild-eyed and magnificent' and, 'like the wilderness itself' (see p.48), she has 'an air of brooding over an inscrutable purpose' (p.87). She is the 'tenebrous and passionate soul' (p.87) of the land and exerts on Kurtz the same mixture of fascination and repulsion. This is obvious when he faces her for the last time and looks at her and all she represents 'with a mingled expression of wistfulness and hate' (p.97). She is unimpressed by the white men and shows the same dignity as the cannibals, as when she alone does not so much as flinch when Marlow pulls the string of the boat's whistle and frightens all the other natives.

The harlequin clearly resents her power and accuses her of trying to persuade Kurtz to kill him (the harlequin). When she opens her arms 'the swift shadows darted out on the earth . . . gathering the steamer into a shadowy embrace' (p.88). This gesture, repeated at the time of departure (p.97), seems to express her attempt to keep possession of

Kurtz's soul, fighting the invisible white muse (the Intended) who struggles for his possession too. Although Marlow is repelled by the unspeakable rites in which his African mistress must have participated with Kurtz, the words he uses to describe her, 'gorgeous', 'magnificent', 'superb', show his admiration for the dynamic energy she symbolises. She too is 'truth stripped of its cloak of time' (p.52), whereas the Intended is all self-deception.

The Intended

She is, like her name, largely symbolical, for she represents the *intention*, the unchanging, absolute idealism men cannot live up to. It is difficult to think of her as a flesh-and-blood woman who loves a real man more than the ideas he expounds. But if we keep in mind what she is supposed to represent, the deadness and illusory greatness of Western civilisation, her presentation is a masterpiece of ambiguity. She has the qualities Marlow most admires: 'A mature capacity for fidelity, for belief, for suffering' (p.106). Marlow reads a 'delicate shade of truthfulness' (p.104) and altruism upon her features. Her surroundings, however, are essentially dead (see the section on 'Imagery' in this Part); she lives in a graveyard supported by a 'saving illusion' (p.108) and a lie. The fact that Marlow should see Kurtz – in his voracious aspect – enter her house with him, and that during their conversation he should see them together and hear the whisper of his last cry, shows that they are indissociable.

For all the clarity of her ideals, Marlow feels he has 'blundered into a place of cruel and absurd mysteries' (p.107). Nowhere better than here does he show that the light she supposedly represents is actually a source of death, as her 'ashy halo' (p.106) suggests. Marlow says that she, too, was just a voice (p.69) and during their interview she 'talked' and 'talked' (p.108). She clearly manoeuvres Marlow into telling her what she wants to hear, and this shows the extent of her self-deception. It is as if she kept the wilderness alive by refusing to recognise its existence. Note the irony at the end of the following passage, in which the words of the girl merge with the reality Kurtz has experienced in the jungle:

> the sound of her low voice seemed to have the accompaniment of all the other sounds, full of mystery, desolation, and sorrow, I had ever heard – the ripple of the river . . . the murmurs of the crowds . . . the whisper of a voice speaking from beyond the threshold of an eternal darkness. "But you have heard him! You know!" she cried. (p.108)

This implies that the light of idealism is inseparable from the darkness of actual life. In the course of the interview the Intended comes increasingly to resemble her opposite, the African mistress. She is possessive like her and exclaims 'he needed me! Me!' (p.110). She too stretches out her arms as after a retreating figure, and her cry of 'inconceivable triumph and unspeakable pain' (p.111) recalls the native woman's 'tragic and fierce aspect' (p.87). Beside her, however, the Intended seems unsubstantial, a mere 'shade' (p.110). We saw that the discrepancy between the idealism she upholds and the darkness of his moral decay is probably part of Kurtz's discovery when he cries out 'The horror! The horror!'. The final irony in the novel (whether intended by Conrad or not, we shall never know) may be that Kurtz's last cry *is* her name and a desperate pronouncement on the spuriousness of one-sided idealism.

The minor characters

The knitters of black wool

Their 'indifferent placidity' and 'unconcerned wisdom' (p.15) disturb Marlow, who feels they know all about him. Their role seems largely symbolical. The older one, 'guarding the door of Darkness . . .' is 'scrutinising the cheery and foolish faces with unconcerned old eyes' (p.16). Marlow thinks of her when he goes ashore after Kurtz (p.93) and is on the point of struggling with the unknown in himself. Because they seem 'uncanny and fateful' (p.16) and knit continuously, they are often taken for the Fates, in classical mythology, goddesses who spin the thread of man's life and determine its course.

The company's clerk

He has a drink with Marlow while they are waiting to go to the doctor's. His sententious comments about those who are foolish enough to go to Africa link him with the petty and ignorant people Marlow meets in the streets of Brussels on his return from Africa.

The doctor

He is a pseudo-scientist, who measures the skulls of those who go 'out there' and finds 'the mental changes of individuals' (p.17) interesting for science, though he never sees the agents when they return. This may mean that he is not interested in seeing them or, ominously, that most do not come back. There is more truth in what he says than he seems to be aware of, particularly in his assertion that 'the changes take place inside'. This implies that each man has inner depths to be explored and that to do so may be dangerous. The mechanical inquiries of the doctor and his obvious indifference to the men under his scrutiny are in keeping with the enterprise he serves and add to Marlow's uneasiness. In the African interior he appropriately remembers the doctor's advice: ' *"Du calme, du calme"* ' (p.17).

The aunt

Her misguided conception of Marlow's 'mission', inspired by what she has read in newspapers and which Marlow calls 'rot' (p.18), has been discussed (see p.35 above). She remains totally impervious to Marlow's assertion that the company is run for profit. Marlow treats her with ironic affection, emphasising her lack of realism which he sees as typical of women: 'It's queer how out of touch with truth women are' (p.18), he says, a statement which also applies to the Intended. To what extent men should help women 'to stay in that beautiful world of their own' (p.69) has been discussed *à propos* Marlow's lie. Her recommendations when Marlow leaves and is 'told to wear flannel, be sure to write often, and so on' (p.18) are ridiculous in the light of the very real moral dangers he faces but of which she is totally unaware.

The structure

The beginning and the end of the novel, presented by a first narrator who introduces Marlow's tale and concludes on it, are usually referred to as the 'frame'. The presentation of a story within the story is a very modern device and has since led to a kind of novel in which a novelist or artist (and, in a sense, Marlow is one) is the hero of his own work of art. One major effect of Conrad's use of a frame and two narrators is to provoke a chain-like reaction: Marlow's story is told to four listeners, one of whom tells it to the readers, who may react differently to it as the listeners do. Among them are a lawyer, an accountant, the company director and the unnamed first narrator. He is the only one who takes part imaginatively in Marlow's tale – and is changed by it, too, as his awareness at the end of the story that the Thames leads 'into the heart of an immense darkness' (p.111) indicates. During one of Marlow's major interruptions he says 'I listened, I listened on the watch for the sentence, for the word, that would give me the clue to the faint uneasiness inspired by this narrative' (p.39). His uneasiness, like Marlow's, is an incentive to *seeing* and understanding the moral significance of Marlow's experience. The other listeners, on the contrary, either sleep through Marlow's tale and thus remain unaware, or do not see what he is driving at, as can be inferred from their reactions (pp.49 and 68). Two of them at least – the company director and the accountant – belong to the same category of men as Marlow meets in Brussels and in Africa, since they also serve commercial interests.

The contrasts it offers with Marlow's point of view serve to highlight the frame of the novel. In spite of the brooding gloom over London, the first narrator uses expressions like 'serenity', 'exquisite brilliance', 'pacifically', 'benign', 'unstained light' (p.6) to describe the end of the day. The optimistic view of colonialism he expresses afterwards matches his view of the landscape. When Marlow says 'And this also . . . has been one of the dark places of the earth', the effect is the more striking and supposes a deeper, imaginative response to his surroundings. So are his comments on the individual's participation in a colonialist expedition: 'imagine the growing regrets, the longing to escape, the powerless disgust, the surrender, the hate' (p.9), words which naturally prefigure Kurtz's predicament. As a matter of fact, the first narrator's introduction raises central issues developed by Marlow's narrative: the dark role of the city as a centre of 'civilisation', the nature of colonialism, the individual's capacity to reflect on it and to explore his own mind.

The division of the narrative into three chapters seems, at first, arbitrary. Each break, however, occurs at a significant moment in Marlow's approach to Kurtz: the first break when he has only heard of him and wonders whether Kurtz is equal to the moral ideas he propounds; the second at the height of Marlow's curiosity about Kurtz just before he discovers what he is really like. Similarly, each pause in the narrative has a specific function and draws attention to Marlow's listeners and their reactions. The first substantial interruption (p.10), for example, elicits from the first narrator his comment on the inconclusiveness of Marlow's experience and awakens the reader's curiosity about the nature of Marlow's tale and therefore of the novel. Another significant pause takes place when one listener has apparently broken it with the exclamation: 'Absurd!' (p.68). Lawrence Graver* writes that this interruption so unnerves Marlow that it leads to a five-page outburst in which he summarises nearly every major theme in the story. Certainly, Marlow sounds emotionally involved, as if he had not wholly digested his experience, when he anticipates his meeting with Kurtz and focuses his attention on the kind of temptation the latter confronted (see pp.68–73).

While making the reader aware of the effect Kurtz has on him, this passage further delays the actual meeting with Kurtz and, like Marlow's other anticipations, adds to the suspense he gradually builds up. At the same time, Marlow's several allusions to Kurtz before his actual appearance in the tale show that Marlow himself proceeds through an association of ideas rather than strictly chronologically. Thanks to this

*In *Conrad's Short Fiction*, University of California Press, Berkeley, 1969, p.79.

method we know all about Kurtz before Marlow relates their meeting; when this takes place, he can concentrate on his struggle with him. In the course of the narrative Marlow's mind moves between the past (the timeless and primeval world he explores) and the future (Kurtz, but also the possible development of any man's mind) and thus illustrates his own assertion that 'the mind of man is capable of anything' (p.52).

Irony

Irony is one of Conrad's favourite methods in this as in other novels. It is a device by which a writer expresses a meaning which contradicts the stated or ostensible one. Its effect in *Heart of Darkness* is to intensify Marlow's indignation and render it more effectively than if he expressed it in so many words. It also provokes in the reader the same reaction as in Marlow. There are several ways of achieving irony. One of them is called 'verbal irony' and occurs when the real meaning of the words is the opposite of that which is literally expressed. Marlow has frequent recourse to it. Referring to the hens over which Fresleven fought and, as a result, was killed, he says 'the cause of progress got them' and calls the affair 'glorious' (p.14), emphasising the futility of the reason for which Fresleven died. He brings out the little serious-ness with which some European nations take their colonising mission by calling colonists on the East Coast of Africa 'the jolly pioneers of progress' (p.15). Marlow's salutation '*Ave!* . . . *Morituri te salutant*' (p.15) points to the discrepancy between the grandiloquent expression and the actual meanness of the enterprise in which he takes part. Calling colonialism 'the merry dance of death and trade' (p.20) or 'high and just proceedings' (p.23); exclaiming 'the work!' (p.24) while meditating over 'the great demoralisation of the land' (p.26), these are so many examples of a contemptuous and incisive verbal irony. Perhaps less obvious but just as effective is the ironic contrast between the colonialists' professions of intention and what they are actually up to; the masterstroke of this kind of irony lies in the contrast between Kurtz's eloquence and the postscript to his report: 'Exterminate all the brutes!' (p.72).

This example is less one of verbal than of dramatic irony, which is conveyed through the structure of a work of art. In the Author's Note to the original edition of the novel Conrad wrote that his 'sombre theme had to be given a sinister resonance . . . a continued vibration that . . . would hang in the air and dwell on the ear after the last note had been struck.' He succeeds in doing so through the pervasive irony of Marlow's narrative, conveyed through a series of parallels, contrasts, and echoes. To the first narrator, for example, the Thames has the 'dignity of a waterway leading to the uttermost ends of the earth' (p.6) but Marlow points out that England too was once 'the end of the world' (p.9). Though not immediately obvious, another parallel is provided between British, Roman and Belgian imperialism since all are 'hunters for gold', robbers or buccaneers. This parallel is clearly part of Conrad's ironic intention since it contrasts with Marlow's remark that 'none of us would feel exactly like this' (p.10). There is an ironic contrast between the darkness at the grove of death and the brightness of the accountant's outfit, between the hardly bearable atmosphere and his saying that he came out 'to get a breath of fresh air' (p.26), between the fact that his books are 'in apple-pie order' while 'Everything else in the station was in a muddle – heads, things, buildings' (p.26). The juxtaposition of 'heads' and 'things' is ironical too. The same kind of ironic contrast is afforded by the efficiency inherent in the old book on seamanship and the utter uselessness of such a book to the harlequin in the jungle. One kind of pervasive irony grows out of the repeated opposition between the littleness of man and the powerful greatness of the landscape. The whisper of Kurtz's last cry echoes through the end of the novel but does so most ironically when Marlow hears it together with the Intended's self-deceived idealistic comments. Conrad's use of parallels and contrasts might be called an associative method. It relies for effect not on explicit statement but, as in poetry, on the reader's capacity to trace these associations. We shall now see that Conrad's ironic method also applies to his use of symbolism and imagery.

Symbolism and imagery

Conrad himself was so much aware of the poetic elements in *Heart of Darkness* that at one stage he was experimenting with his narrative and scanning it into blank verse. It could be demonstrated, however, that this novel is poetic in its very conception and that practically every element in its literary structure contributes to its symbolism.

The title is symbolical and covers a psychological as much as a geographical reality. It refers to the ambivalent force at the heart of the wilderness; it also stands for the central darkness Kurtz discovers within himself, and possibly at the heart of all civilised consciousness. The title indirectly alludes to the setting, which is also symbolical. The use of Africa as an inner, unknown, territory was not new. As early a writer as Sir Thomas Browne (1605–82) wrote in *Religio Medici* (1642): 'We carry within us the wonders we seek without us: there is all Africa and her prodigies in us'. Saul Bellow (*b*.1915), a contemporary American writer, wrote in *Henderson the Rain King* (1959): 'Well, maybe every guy has his own Africa'. The plot of *Heart of Darkness*, the voyage from Outer to Central to Inner Station, symbolises a journey into the self. If we think of Marlow's voice reaching his listeners in the growing darkness from the depths of his consciousness, the very telling of the tale becomes symbolical of an inner voyage. The actual journey offers all through a second level of interpretation. Critics have read in it a descent into man's unconscious or into an underworld recalling similar episodes in the *Aeneid,* an epic poem by Virgil (70–19BC), or in the *Divine Comedy* by Dante (1265–1321), or in the Orpheus legend. It has also been suggested that Marlow's journey stands for the quest of the grail originally told in medieval legends. This interpretation would naturally apply to Marlow's quest of Kurtz, not to the manager's agents. Indeed, when Marlow uses words with a religious connotation such as 'pilgrims', 'god' or 'pray', he is strongly ironical and merely implies that the manager and his followers have deified their commercial interests.

The characters, too, are symbolical. Kurtz can be looked upon as Marlow's shadow, and when Marlow first meets him, he seems to be coming up from the ground (p.84). The natives at the grove of death are like phantoms in hell. The native mistress represents the African soul while the Intended stands for the idealism of Western civilisation. The painting by Kurtz in the brickmaker's hut 'representing a woman, draped and blindfolded, carrying a lighted torch' (p.36) seems to symbolise both the 'idea' and the Intended. It is strongly ironical since, in spite of the torch she carries, the woman cannot see. Other objects Marlow comes across carry a symbolical meaning: the derelict machinery at the Outer Station points to the destructive impact of Africa on what has been created by white civilisation. Most impressive, however, is the symbolism of the landscape descriptions. To take but one example, Marlow describes the effect of the jungle on him one night at the Central Station:

> The great wall of vegetation, an exuberant and entangled mass of trunks, branches, leaves, boughs, festoons, motionless in the moonlight, was like a rioting invasion of soundless life, a rolling wave of plants, piled up, crested, ready to topple over the creek, to sweep every little man of us out of his little existence. (p.43)

Conrad uses a sea image ('a rolling wave . . . crested . . . ready to topple') to convey the sense of threatening engulfment Marlow experiences, and to foreshadow the impact of the jungle on Kurtz. Taken together, however, Conrad's poetic descriptions of the African interior create a dense and populated inner landscape at the heart of every man's consciousness.

The 'light and darkness' imagery pervades the narrative and is one of Conrad's most effective tools in conveying his meaning. Conventional symbolism associates light and white with good, black with evil.

Conrad mostly departs from this connotation, and even when he adheres to it, he does so in a subtle and complex way. At the beginning of the novel light shines on the Thames estuary, whereas a brooding gloom envelops London. The brooding gloom is mentioned five times in three pages. It is the more ironical as London, 'the greatest town on earth' (p.5), is the greatest centre of progress and that it is from here that 'bearers of a spark from the sacred fire' of civilisation (p.7) start. The sun over the estuary is 'striken to death' (p.6) by the touch of the gloom over the city, a powerful image suggesting that men are responsible for the darkness in the world. The phrase 'a brooding gloom in sunshine' (p.7) sums up the theme of the novel, the existence of darkness at the core of a shining civilisation; it is echoed by a similar image at the Inner Station: 'All this [Kurtz's hut and the heads on poles] was in the gloom, while we down there were yet in the sunshine' (p.84). The sunlight at the Outer Station is 'blinding' (p.22), and the accountant is a blind man indeed. Here all that is associated with light and the white man, the symbolical piece of white worsted around the neck of a dying slave, the accountant's shining outfit, is a source of appalling darkness and suggests a complete reversal of values. The torch-light on Kurtz's painting has a sinister effect. The postscript to Kurtz's report is 'luminous and terrifying, like a flash of lightning in a serene sky' (p.72) and blazes with a light of destruction. Most ironical of all is the association of light and darkness during Marlow's interview with the Intended. The windows in the room, normally a source of light, are 'luminous and bedraped columns' (p.106) as in a mortuary. The 'cold and monumental whiteness' of the fireplace adds to the deathlike atmosphere. While the Intended talks, her forehead 'illumined by the unextinguishable light of belief and love' (p.107), the darkness in the room deepens as if to contradict her words, and this recalls the ambivalence of Kurtz's gift of eloquence: 'the pulsating stream of light, or the deceitful flow from the heart of an impenetrable darkness' (p.68).

Images of death also abound in the novel, linking the white men's activities in the metropolis with their actions in the wilderness. Brussels is twice compared to a sepulchre (pp.14 and 102). The company headquarters are 'a house in the city of the dead' (p.16). The Intended's house is in a street like 'a well-kept alley in a cemetery' (p.105), and the piano in her drawing-room is like a 'sarcophagus' (p.106). These images intimate that she too is at the source of the deadly enterprise. Both blacks and whites are its victims. We can visualise the 'massacre' of blacks reduced to 'phantoms' at the grove of death but Kurtz, himself 'an animated image of death' (p.85), is both its agent and its victim. The comparison of the accountant to a 'hair-dresser's dummy' (p.26) and of the brickmaker's eyes to 'mica discs'

(p.35) express death through dehumanisation. So does the transformation of men into 'raw matter' (p.23). The pilgrims' greed for
ivory generates death: 'A taint of imbecile rapacity blew through it
all, like a whiff from some corpse' (p.33). The association between
ivory and death is even clearer in the macabre juxtaposition that
suggests itself between the 'ivory ball' (p.69) of Kurtz's head and the
'black, dried, sunken' (p.82) ball of the head on the pole. There are
other images less obviously connected with death but equally sug-
gestive of the destructive or futile presence of the white man in Africa.
The hole is one of them. There is the purposeless 'vast artificial hole'
(p.23) at the grove of death, the hole in the pail the pilgrim uses to stop
the fire at the Central Station; the manager has made a hole in the
bottom of the steamer on some rocks, thus delaying the rescue of
Kurtz and possibly hastening his death. The growing grass invading
the remains of men and of their achievements is another recurring
image, an ironic comment on the evanescence of human existence.

Style

The parallels and contrasts in the narrative, its symbolism and imagery,
are aspects of style – the unique or specific verbal pattern a writer uses
to express his meaning. Conrad's style in *Heart of Darkness* is marked
by repetitions which have a cumulative effect and also contribute to
the 'vibration' which, so he hoped, would still impress the reader after
closing the book. Another musical characteristic of his writing is his
frequent use of alliteration as in the 'slimy swell swung' (p.20). He
sometimes creates a weird effect by giving a voice to the landscape
itself only referring implicitly to the men in it as in 'the mist itself had
screamed' (p.57), 'the bush began to howl' (p.65) or 'a weird incanta-
tion came out of the black, flat wall of the woods' (p.92).

One objection sometimes jars with the chorus of approval of
Conrad's style: it bears on his frequent use of adjectives such as
'impenetrable', 'inconceivable', or 'inscrutable'. F.R. Leavis* wrote
that Conrad 'is intent on making a virtue out of not knowing what he
means'. Several arguments have been used to counter this opinion.
Generally, they are to the effect that Marlow does mean to convey his
bewilderment in the face of the mysteriousness of what he describes
and to draw attention to its inexpressibility. Conrad himself claimed
'an inalienable right to the use of all my epithets', a proof, if necessary,
that they are part of his artistic purpose.

The Great Tradition, Chatto & Windus, London, 1948, p.199.

The resonance of *Heart of Darkness*

Conrad's hope that the resonance of his novel would hang in the air long after the last note had been struck has been more than fulfilled, not with individual readers alone but through decade after decade. *Heart of Darkness* has probably received, and continues to receive, as much critical attention as any work of fiction in English. But it has taken some time for all its aspects and levels of meaning to be fully appreciated. When it was first published, Edward Garnett (1865–1937), a man of letters and a contemporary of Conrad, gave it a very intelligent and perceptive review. Some readers, however, were puzzled by it or praised it for the wrong reasons. It was only gradually that critics found ever new possibilities of interpretation.

What is perhaps most interesting is to see how readers of the Third World now react to *Heart of Darkness*. The Nigerian novelist Chinua Achebe (*b.*1930) severely criticises Conrad for merely adopting what he says was the dominant image of Africa in the Western imagination. He writes that Conrad presents Africa as 'a place of negations . . . in comparison with which Europe's own state of spiritual grace will be manifest'. He sees the novel as a racist work in which 'the very humanity of black people is called in question'. Ngugi Wa Thiong'o (*b.*1938), the Kenyan writer, partly agrees with Achebe but thinks that he overlooked Conrad's attack on colonialism. The African critic C.P. Sarvan has shown that contrary to what Achebe wrote, Conrad – though not wholly immune from the attitudes of his age – was ahead of people in trying to break free from those attitudes. It is the Guyanese novelist Wilson Harris (*b.*1921) who has written the most sensitive and imaginative vindication of *Heart of Darkness*. He calls it a 'frontier novel', by which he means that Conrad arrived upon a frontier of imagination which he never crossed, though to reach it was an extraordinary achievement. Through a close analysis of the imagery Harris argues that Conrad went a considerable way towards recognising the 'otherness' of the African people and broke with the 'uniform prejudice' that prevailed at the turn of the twentieth century.

Within the British Commonwealth new writers have written novels in the same tradition as *Heart of Darkness*, which recreate similar experiences as Marlow's. It is worth singling out *Palace of the Peacock* (1960) by Wilson Harris, *A Fringe of Leaves* (1976) by the Australian Nobel Prize winner Patrick White (*b.*1912), and *A Bend in the River* (1979) by the Trinidadian V.S. Naipaul (*b.*1932). This could, in fact, be considered as a follow-up to *Heart of Darkness*.

Part 4

Hints for study

Heart of Darkness is a short but complex novel of an inexhaustible richness. It can be read an unlimited number of times and each new reading is likely to yield new shades of meaning. If you approach it for the first time, you will see that it is a novel about colonialism; you will be able to follow Marlow's journey into the African interior; but you may well ask yourself questions about Marlow's disquisitions on human behaviour and the significance of his meeting with Kurtz. You are advised to read the novel once for pleasure and interest, and a second time with the help of the notes and glossaries provided in Part 2 of this study, to make sure you understand its literal meaning. The subsequent reading(s) will involve a systematic survey of all the elements that make up the form of the novel, and are indissociable from its content. You may be able to combine stages two and three. But remember that the novel demands serious and thoughtful consideration.

One golden rule in literary analysis is never to take for granted another reader's or critic's interpretation of a text. Criticism is meant to help you, not to replace your own thinking. In forming your own opinion, however, always make sure that it is substantiated by the text.

Reading method

We have referred in Part 3 to Conrad's associative method, which requires the reader's participation to discern the ironic parallels and contrasts by which meaning is conveyed.

Prepare the outlines of a master-sheet that you will fill in as you read the story for the second or third time. The master-sheet should be divided up into sections, each representing one *character*, one major *idea* Marlow discusses, one major *aspect of the novel*. Proceed systematically and do not try to fill in all the sections in one reading. You will have a section on Marlow and one on Kurtz. For example:

Characters: Kurtz

p.27. *The accountant:* 'In the interior you will no doubt meet Mr Kurtz. . . . He is a very remarkable person'.

p.36. *The brickmaker:* 'He is a prodigy. . . . He is an emissary of light, and science, and progress'.

p.40. *The brickmaker:* 'Mr Kurtz was a "universal genius" '.
p.45. *The manager:* 'He has asked the Administration to be sent there . . . with the idea of showing what he could do. . . . Look at the influence that man must have. . . . Ivory . . . lots of it . . . most annoying from him'.

When you have written down all that has been said about Kurtz and by whom, you will gradually form your own picture of him and will be able to write a character sketch of him. You will have to interpret what is said according to whom the speaker is. The accountant and the harlequin are sincere when they express admiration for Kurtz. The manager is frankly envious when talking to his uncle about him, but a hypocrite when he addresses Marlow. Compare the portrait you have formed of Kurtz with Marlow's impressions before and after his meeting with him.

In a letter to the *New York Times* written in 1901 Conrad refers to the fundamental influences that inform all human behaviour, and consequently art, as 'egoism, which is the moving force of the world, and altruism, which is its morality'; he further alludes to 'their ir-reconcilable antagonism'. If you are asked to write an essay on Kurtz, show to what extent he is ridden by these contradictory forces and the consequences of his incapacity to reconcile them. Also, explain the journalist's statement about him, 'He could get himself to believe any-thing – anything. . . . He was an – an – extremist' (p.104), and show how it is illustrated in the novel.

Your section on Marlow is likely to be the most difficult one. Put down your impressions as they arise from what he says. His tone varies considerably in the course of the narrative. He is by turn matter-of-fact, indignant, humorous, ironical. From the tone he uses, determine the intention behind his words.

In Part 3 it was suggested that Marlow has a little in common with most other characters but was not demonstrated systematically. Find examples of this. Not everything has been said about him. To what extent, for example, does he illustrate the values of courage and fidelity Conrad so much appreciated?

Marlow has been called a potential Kurtz. To what extent is this true?

Explain in your own terms Marlow's mixture of sympathy for, and revulsion of, Kurtz.

There are several contradictions in Marlow. Point out those we have not referred to already.

Finally, try to determine how far Marlow can be identified with Conrad himself. In trying to answer this question you will have to take into account not only Conrad's own experience in the Congo, but also the circumstances in which Conrad might not wish to identify with his character. For example, what do you make of Marlow's nervousness when his shoes are full of blood? Does it indicate a lack of self-control on his part?

Ideas: Reality – Truth / Unreality – Dream

Attention has been drawn above to Conrad's dual presentation of reality as well as to his sense of the unreal. But the subject is far from exhausted. In this section have two columns in which you will list all passages dealing with what Marlow calls real and unreal. For example:

p.19: 'Now and then a boat from the shore gave one a momentary contact with reality'.
p.33: 'I've never seen anything so unreal in my life'.
p.35: 'It was as unreal as everything else'.
p.37: 'The amazing reality of [the land's] concealed life'.
p.39: 'It seems to me I'm trying to tell you a dream'.
p.41: 'I like what is in the work . . . your own reality'.
p.48: 'The overwhelming realities of this strange world of plants'.
p.48: '[one's past] came in the shape of an unrestful and noisy dream'.
p.49: 'The reality – the reality . . . fades'.

When your list is complete on both sides, compare the various meanings of reality; compare the various meanings of unreality; then contrast the notions of reality and unreality you will have arrived at.

Similarly, devote a section to the notions of efficiency/inefficiency, restraint/lack of restraint, enigma, darkness (compare the darkness over which the two women keep watch in Brussels with the darkness to which the manager's uncle appeals in the jungle. Does Marlow mean by it the same thing as when he talks of Kurtz's 'impenetrable darkness'?). See also what Marlow means by 'idea', as in 'What redeems it is the idea' (p.10).

You may discover other notions that are worth explaining. When you have done so, you will find it easier to define what may be referred to as Marlow's 'philosophy'.

Symbolism

Heart of Darkness has been called the first symbolist novel in English, and this applies as much to its imagery as to its general conception and the levels of meaning it elicits.

Conrad himself saw the *image* as the fittest instrument of the imagination to render what was most essential in a human being. To a fellow writer he said 'you must search the darkest corners of your heart, the most remote recesses of your brain, – you must search them for the image, for the glamour, for the right expression'. He also revealed that in writing this novel he did not start with an abstract notion: 'I start with definite images'.

Part 3 has indicated in what way the imagery contributes to the overall meaning of the novel. But the discussion is far from exhaustive. On your master-sheet (prepare a second or a third, if necessary) devote a section to the religious imagery, to the light and darkness imagery which has not been discussed above, and to images of death. In his preface to *The Secret Agent* Conrad calls London 'a cruel devourer of the world's light'. How does this image of the big city apply to London and Brussels in *Heart of Darkness?*

Some images have not been discussed at all in Part 3; for example, the river is several times compared to a snake or a demon, while Marlow sees himself as a 'silly little bird' (p.12) charmed by it. How does the river image function? What do snake and bird stand for? What do these images add to the meaning of the text? You might devote a section on your master-sheet to all the images that have not been discussed and determine likewise in what way they contribute to the general meaning of the novel.

The *landscape* descriptions matter very much in a poetic novel of this kind. They are an essential aspect of its symbolical and even metaphysical content, since the link between man and his environment is so significant. Only one such description has been discussed in these Notes. Make a survey of all landscape descriptions and show how they add meaning to Marlow's experience. See, in particular, p.56 – the passage from 'the current ran smooth and swift' to 'a very loud cry . . . soared slowly in the opaque air'. Examine its elements carefully. What particular effect does the whole create?

One long passage which also requires a detailed analysis runs from 'At last we opened a reach' (p.21) to 'which were in apple-pie order' (p.26). It is not only a landscape description; it shows how colonialism spoils the environment and disrupts the society of the native population. This is an epitome of Marlow's discoveries about colonialism in Africa. Write an essay about it, showing on a limited scale how all the elements make up the narrative function: characterisation, imagery, irony. Show also in what way Conrad sees living creatures reduced to matter while the inanimate is personalised.

Specimen answer: Colonialism

When Marlow reaches the Outer Station, the misgivings he has had in Brussels and on his journey along the African coast are confirmed.

He is deeply shocked by what he discovers, although he does not convey his reaction in indignant tones but gives a minute description of what he sees, which in turn shocks the reader into an awareness of the effects of the white man's presence in Africa.

The land is laid waste by a series of explosions which disfigure it needlessly, for they are ineffective and take place on cliffs that are not even an obstacle to the intended railway. Phrases such as 'mounds of turned-up-earth', 'a waste of excavations' and 'inhabited devastation' create a striking picture of destructiveness. 'Objectless blasting' emphasises the futility of the white men's enterprise, a futility increased by the decay of the machinery they have imported and the impression of disorder and chaos it creates. The boiler 'wallowing in the grass', the railway-truck 'lying . . . on its back with its wheels in the air' and looking 'as dead as the carcass of some animal' are presented as used-up living creatures now discarded and dead. They add up to the general lifelessness of the setting.

Worse even than the devastated land is the degree of dehumanisation Marlow witnesses in the men he encounters. The first group consists of slaves each with an iron collar on his neck and all linked together by a chain. They are called criminals, just as the natives fired at from the man-of-war were called enemies, in order to justify the way they are being treated. The slaves are reduced to an animal-like state that is suggested by the black rags waggling 'to and fro like tails'. Their stony stare and appearance of 'deathlike indifference' reveal in fact their despair, of which Marlow alone seems to be aware. He calls them 'dark things' and 'raw matter'. Yet the horror he experiences only reaches a climax when he comes upon natives too tired or too ill to work and merely left to die in the 'greenish gloom' of the forest. Again, the words used to describe men – 'shapes', 'bundles of acute angles', 'phantoms' – eloquently express the fact that they have been reduced to mere objects, squeezed out of life through hard labour, then discarded. Just as the setting offers a picture of devastation, so the condition and posture of the men suggest 'a massacre or a pestilence'. It is this prevalence of death among men in the ravaged forest that gives Marlow the impression that he has entered some gloomy inferno. All this time in the background he hears the 'continuous' and 'rushing' noise of the rapids, the symbol of a force which, for all his destructive impact, the white man cannot conquer.

Marlow's indignation is conveyed not by his tone, but rather through his irony. The so-called criminals punished by the 'outraged law', the blacks dying of disease and starvation brought 'in all the legality of time contracts', point to the hypocrisy of the white man's enterprise. Marlow is ironical towards both the system and himself when he says 'I also was a part of the great cause of these high and just proceedings'.

He becomes more sarcastic when he sees a vast hole possibly connected, as he suggests, 'with the philanthropic desire of giving the criminals something to do'. There is also irony in his juxtaposition of 'the work!' (meaning the white man's enterprise) and his reference to the place where some of the helpers have withdrawn to die. The best example of dramatic irony, however, lies in the contrast between the grove of death and the image of light provided by the accountant. In spite of Marlow's admiration for his achievement, we realise that his is not the true light of civilisation but mere external appearance. He is himself like a dead man, a 'hairdresser's dummy', and we are horrified by the insensitiveness of a man whose books are 'in apple-pie order' yet is blind to the surrounding 'inferno' to the extent of coming out 'to get a breath of fresh air' amid the dying.

Taken as a whole, this passage illustrates the reality of colonialism at its worst. As Marlow's insistence on blackness, disease, and death indicates, it is not light but darkness the white man has brought with him, unless it be the false light radiated by the accountant. The light of the land is repeatedly called blinding and seems to have rendered the white man unaware of what he is really up to. The evil Marlow has suspected on the voyage out takes here a definite shape, and he now sees that he will become acquainted 'with a flabby, pretending, weak-eyed devil of a rapacious and pitiless folly'.

Irony

You will have noticed in Part 3 above how often irony is mentioned. Again, the subject is far from exhausted, and you will not really understand the novel unless you see for yourself how irony functions in it. Find examples of verbal irony; there are many. When, for example, Marlow says 'their extravagant salary . . . was paid with the regularity of a large and honourable trading company' (p.59), ask yourself what in this sentence makes Marlow's statement ironical.

Language

George Orwell (1903–50), in his novel *1984* (1949), shows how language can be corrupted for political purposes. Long before him Conrad showed the same in *Heart of Darkness*. See, for example, the way in which the natives are called 'criminals', 'enemies', 'rebels'. Can you find other examples of language used for the purpose of political exploitation?

There is also a lot of black humour in the novel. For instance, Marlow calls the pilgrims 'unwholesome' and 'unappetising' (p.59). Can you find other examples?

Note also Marlow's frequent juxtapositions of opposites as in 'diabolic love' and 'unearthly hate' (p.98). Can you find other examples and explain their effect?

Themes

Only the major theme has been mentioned in passing in Part 3. If you have read this part carefully and have read the novel according to our suggestions, you should now be able to bring to light its many sub-themes and motifs. You may also want to give your own definition of what you consider the main theme.

Interpretation

Two incidents have given rise to countless interpretations. They are Kurtz's cry 'The horror! The horror!' and Marlow's lie. Give your own interpretation of each. Make sure you substantiate your answer and that it fits in with what you know – and can demonstrate – of Kurtz and Marlow. With regard to Marlow's lie, remember in particular one comment of his which has not been discussed in these Notes: 'I laid the ghost of his gifts at last with a lie' (p.69). What does he mean by this?

Heart of Darkness has been explained:

(a) As a 'night journey' or a story of initiation, in which man moves from innocence to experience, and appreciates good all the more as he has become acquainted with the nature of evil. That Marlow acquires such wisdom is suggested by the picture of him at the end sitting 'apart, indistinct and silent, in the pose of a meditating Buddha' (p.111).

(b) As a political satire.

(c) As a quest which presents all the aspects of an adventure story as of a knight in search of an 'enchanted princess sleeping in a fabulous castle' (p.61) or of a pilgrim in search of the grail.

(d) As a mythological descent into Hell, with Marlow as the equivalent of a mythic hero bringing back the light from his trip into darkness. Think of the women in black guarding the door to the unknown; of the grove of death; the dream-like atmosphere; the black shapes in the forest; Kurtz appearing as from the ground (p.84); the red gleams as Kurtz goes ashore, and so on.

(e) As a journey into the unconscious, that is, into the darkness of the inner self over which man normally maintains conscious control. Kurtz achieves complete freedom and gains access to his unconscious. Marlow has access to his through Kurtz, but remains in control of his inner self.

Choose the interpretation which you think most valid or in which you are most interested. Pick out all the elements that sustain such an interpretation and write an essay about it. Make sure your essay forms a consistent whole including a logical development of your arguments and a conclusion.

Specimen answer: journey into the unconscious

Heart of Darkness can be interpreted as a journey into the unconscious. This implies that the individual is deprived of the usual support of society and must rely on his own inner strength, as Marlow puts it, for moral and spiritual support. He is confronted with a dimension of existence or inner forces which, in his normal state, he manages to control. These mysterious and normally repressed forces can be considered as the essence of the self, which manifests itself in dreams or when man is in a state of strain. It links man with the primordial and the unknown in the universe. The unconscious acts as an incentive to our actions and thoughts, both good and evil.

That Marlow might be setting on a journey into the unconscious is already suggested by the doctor who tells him that 'the changes take place inside' (p.17). On the voyage out, Africa is presented as an enigma, a continent which might stand for an inner reality to be explored 'smiling, frowning, inviting, grand, mean, insipid, or savage, and always mute, with an air of whispering, Come and find out' (p.19). At the Central Station, he feels 'its mystery, its greatness, the amazing reality of its concealed life' (p.37). When he sets out for the interior to meet Kurtz, he says 'going up that river was like travelling back to the earliest beginning of the world' (p.48). There is thus a repeated emphasis on his voyage as an exploration of the mysterious and the primordial, the 'rioting invasion of soundless life' (p.43). This is enhanced by the impressive muteness of the land, occasionally broken by the wild noises of the natives, and by the sense of unreality and dream Marlow experiences as he travels further into the interior.

The man who is incapable of controlling his unconscious runs the danger of becoming mad, and this is clearly illustrated in the novel. The faithless pilgrims are in no such danger because, as Marlow points out, they are hollow inside. They are amoral beings who can neither be fulfilled nor destroyed since they are empty, dehumanised characters to begin with. Marlow, on the contrary, has sufficient consciousness to be aware of the danger he faces and realises he is often tempted to give in to the wilderness outside and within him. When, for example, he thinks he will have rivets, he momentarily loses his self-control and behaves like a lunatic with the foreman. During the journey up-river he responds to the 'incomprehensible frenzy' of the natives, 'an

enthusiastic outbreak in a madhouse' (p.51); he acknowledges his
kinship with the natives and his desire to 'go ashore for a howl and a
dance' (p.52), from which he is prevented by lack of time and the need
to attend to his work.

It is in Kurtz, however, that the confrontation with the unconscious
is fully illustrated. Marlow points out that Kurtz has undergone 'some
devilish initiation' (p.69), and the harlequin tells Marlow that Kurtz
would 'forget himself' (p.81) among the natives. By thus forgetting
himself, Kurtz has come face to face with his unconscious and achieved
complete freedom. Marlow never reaches such complete freedom
himself but becomes a privileged spectator of it in Kurtz, and his
struggle with Kurtz when he goes ashore after him is in a sense a
struggle to preserve his own balance and sanity: 'I tried to break . . . the
heavy, mute spell of the wilderness – that seemed to draw him [Kurtz]
to its pitiless breast by the awakening of forgotten and brutal instincts'
(p.94). Kurtz has 'kicked himself loose of the earth' (p.95). His soul
'had looked within itself, and . . . it had gone mad'. 'I had . . . to go
through the ordeal of looking into it myself' (p.95), says Marlow.
Though it has freed him, the complete knowledge Kurtz has achieved
by looking into himself has made him totally destructive, as the postscript to his pamphlet ('Exterminate all the brutes') indicates. But it
has destroyed him in turn, and he understands this when he exclaims
'The horror! The horror!' (p.100). Marlow also has felt the power of
the wilderness but above all he has felt its power over Kurtz, with
whom he struggles as with an *alter ego*. The difference between the two
men is that Marlow has exercised throughout his journey, and at the
climax of it, a restraint of which Kurtz has been incapable.

When Marlow returns to society he has gained knowledge of his own
self and of man's capacity for evil. It is this that makes it difficult for
him to adjust to a society ignorant of its limitations as well as of the
creative possibilities to which self-knowledge gives access.

Suggestions for essay topics

You will find below a list of quotations from the novel. Each of them
sums up, directly or indirectly, one of its major aspects. Each can
serve as the starting point of a short essay, for which you will find all
the elements in the novel itself. For example, if you deal with subject
(d), pick out the many passages in which Conrad presents different
kinds of folly or sheer madness. Marlow himself says he and the
foreman behaved like lunatics when they thought they would have
rivets (p.42). Shortly afterwards he talks of the 'folly' of the El Dorado
explorers (p.43). Commenting on human behaviour in general he says
'Of course you may be too much of a fool to go wrong . . . I take it, no

fool ever made a bargain for his soul with the devil: the fool is too much of a fool, or the devil too much of a devil'. About Kurtz he says 'his soul was mad . . . it had looked within itself, and . . . it had gone mad' (p.95).

What difference does Marlow make between folly and madness? Show in what way each is illustrated in the novel. In your argument you will have to connect your illustration of folly and/or madness with what you consider as the main theme of the novel. In your conclusion you will have to show what the discussion of this subject reveals about Conrad's view of men.

(a) 'We live in the flicker – may it last as long as the old earth keeps rolling!' (p.8).

(b) 'Land in a swamp, march through the woods, and in some inland post feel the savagery . . . all that mysterious life that stirs in the forest, in the jungles, in the heart of wild men' (p.9).

(c) 'The conquest of the earth, which mostly means the taking it away from those who have a different complexion or slightly flatter noses than ourselves, is not a pretty thing when you look into it too much. What redeems it is the idea only. An idea at the back of it; not a sentimental pretence but an idea . . . something you can set up, and bow down before, and offer a sacrifice to . . .' (p.10).

(d) 'I foresaw that in the blinding sunshine of that land I would become acquainted with a flabby, pretending, weak-eyed devil of a rapacious and pitiless folly' (p.23).

(e) 'The earth for us is a place to live in . . . breathe dead hippo, so to speak, and not be contaminated. And there . . . your strength comes in, the faith in your ability for the digging of unostentatious holes to bury the stuff in' (p.71).

(f) 'I confounded the beat of the drum with the beating of my heart' (p.93).

(g) '[the] secular trees look[ed] patiently after [the steamer], this grimy fragment of another world, the forerunner of change, of conquest, of trade, of massacres, of blessings' (p.98).

(h) 'Droll thing life is – that mysterious arrangement of merciless logic for a futile purpose. The most you can hope from it is some knowledge of yourself – that comes too late – a crop of unextinguishable regrets' (p.100).

A further suggestion for your consideration

'Once and for all and for ever, let us have done with the ugly imperialism of any absolute' (D.H. Lawrence).

Part 5

Suggestions for further reading

The text

These Notes refer to pages in the Penguin Books Edition, Penguin Books, Harmondsworth, 1973; reprinted 1977. The Everyman paperback edition, Dent, London, 1967, has an introduction and notes.

Other works by Joseph Conrad

Almayer's Folly, 1895
An Outcast of the Islands, 1896
The Nigger of the Narcissus, 1898
An Outpost of Progress, 1898
Lord Jim, 1900
Youth, 1902
Typhoon, 1903
Nostromo, 1904

The Secret Agent, 1907
Under Western Eyes, 1911
The Secret Sharer, 1912
Chance, 1913
Victory, 1915
The Shadow-line, 1917
Tales of Hearsay, 1925

This list is not exhaustive. All the novels and stories are published by Dent and Penguin.

Autobiographies and letters

The Mirror of the Sea; Memories and Impressions, Methuen, London, 1906.
A Personal Record (first published as *Some Reminiscences*), Nash, London, 1912.
AUBRY, G.J.: *Joseph Conrad; Life and Letters*, 2 vols., Doubleday, Garden City, New York, 1927.

Background reading

DAICHES, DAVID: *The Novel and the Modern World*, The University of Chicago Press, Chicago, 1960. Contains a good chapter on Conrad whom he considers the first important modern novelist in English. Also deals with James Joyce, D.H. Lawrence and Virginia Woolf.

FORD, BORIS (ED.): *The Pelican Guide to English Literature* (No.7), Penguin Books, Harmondsworth, 1961. Describes the social and intellectual background as well as the literary scene in Conrad's time. Contains a perceptive chapter by Douglas Brown: 'From *Heart of Darkness* to *Nostromo*: An Approach to Conrad'.

LEAVIS, F.R.: *The Great Tradition*, Chatto & Windus, London, 1948. Re-issued in a paperback edition in association with Penguin Books, Hardmondsworth, 1962. Places Conrad within the great tradition of the English novel. Praises *Nostromo* but criticises the repetition of adjectives in *Heart of Darkness*, an objection repeatedly echoed by subsequent critics.

SHERRY, NORMAN: *Conrad and his World*, Thames & Hudson, London, 1972. Largely biographical; well illustrated.

Studies of Conrad

BAINES, JOCELYN: Joseph Conrad, *A Critical Biography*, Weidenfeld & Nicolson, London, 1960; also Penguin Books, Harmondsworth, 1971. The standard biography of Conrad. Contains an informative chapter on the 'Congo Episode' in Conrad's life, an analysis of *Heart of Darkness*, and of Marlow's role in Conrad's stories.

BERTHOUD, JACQUES: *Joseph Conrad: the Major Phase*, Cambridge University Press, Cambridge, 1978. Contains an excellent chapter on *Heart of Darkness*.

COX, C.B.: *Joseph Conrad: the Modern Imagination*, Dent, London, 1974. The chapter on *Heart of Darkness* sums up other critics' interpretations and discusses the main themes and the technique of the novel. Suitable for the more advanced student.

FLEISHMAN, AVROM: *Conrad's Politics*, Johns Hopkins Press, Baltimore, 1967. Concentrates on the disruptive effects of imperialism on native society in *Heart of Darkness*.

GEKOSKI, R.A.: *Conrad, The Moral World of the Novelist,* Paul Elek, London, 1978. Presents *Heart of Darkness* as a significant illustration of Conrad's moral vision.

GRAVER, LAWRENCE: *Conrad's Short Fiction,* University of California Press, Berkeley, 1969. The section on *Heart of Darkness* contains a very good discussion of the 'frame' in that novel.

GUERARD, ALBERT: *Conrad the Novelist*, Harvard University Press, Cambridge, Mass., 1958. Remains one of the best studies on Conrad. First presented *Heart of Darkness* as a 'night journey'.

SHERRY, NORMAN: *Conrad's Western World,* Cambridge University Press, Cambridge, 1971. Offers a detailed discussion of the sources of *Heart of Darkness, Nostromo* and *The Secret Agent.* Contains many interesting and relevant illustrations.

Recent articles

ACHEBE, CHINUA: 'An Image of Africa', *Research in African Literatures*, 9 (Spring 1978), pp.1–15; and 'Viewpoint', *Times Literary Supplement*, 1 February 1980, p.113. Both articles strongly criticise Conrad for what Achebe considers his racist attitude to Africans.

HARRIS, WILSON: 'The Frontier on which *Heart of Darkness* Stands', *Explorations, A Selection of Talks and Articles*, Dangaroo Press, Aarhus, 1981. Answers Achebe's objections. Offers an original and illuminating interpretation of *Heart of Darkness*.

The author of these notes

HENA MAES-JELINEK has a BA degree from an American University and a PhD from the University of Liège, Belgium. She is *chargé de cours* in English Literature at the University of Liège and was a visiting professor at the University of Abidjan (Ivory Coast). Her books include *Criticism of Society in the English Novel between the Wars* (1970), *The Naked Design* (1976), *Wilson Harris* (a study of his novels to be published in 1981), and a book of essays, *Commonwealth Literature and the Modern World* (1975). Most of her articles are on the English and the Commonwealth novel.

York Notes: list of titles

CHINUA ACHEBE
A Man of the People
Arrow of God
Things Fall Apart

EDWARD ALBEE
Who's Afraid of Virginia Woolf?

ELECHI AMADI
The Concubine

ANONYMOUS
Beowulf
Everyman

AYI KWEI ARMAH
The Beautyful Ones Are Not Yet Born

W. H. AUDEN
Selected Poems

JANE AUSTEN
Emma
Mansfield Park
Northanger Abbey
Persuasion
Pride and Prejudice
Sense and Sensibility

HONORÉ DE BALZAC
Le Père Goriot

SAMUEL BECKETT
Waiting for Godot

SAUL BELLOW
Henderson, The Rain King

ARNOLD BENNETT
Anna of the Five Towns
The Card

WILLIAM BLAKE
Songs of Innocence, Songs of Experience

ROBERT BOLT
A Man For All Seasons

HAROLD BRIGHOUSE
Hobson's Choice

ANNE BRONTË
The Tenant of Wildfell Hall

CHARLOTTE BRONTË
Jane Eyre

EMILY BRONTË
Wuthering Heights

ROBERT BROWNING
Men and Women

JOHN BUCHAN
The Thirty-Nine Steps

JOHN BUNYAN
The Pilgrim's Progress

BYRON
Selected Poems

GEOFFREY CHAUCER
Prologue to the Canterbury Tales
The Clerk's Tale
The Franklin's Tale
The Knight's Tale
The Merchant's Tale
The Miller's Tale
The Nun's Priest's Tale
The Pardoner's Tale
The Wife of Bath's Tale
Troilus and Criseyde

SAMUEL TAYLOR COLERIDGE
Selected Poems

SIR ARTHUR CONAN DOYLE
The Hound of the Baskervilles

WILLIAM CONGREVE
The Way of the World

JOSEPH CONRAD
Heart of Darkness
Nostromo
Victory

STEPHEN CRANE
The Red Badge of Courage

BRUCE DAWE
Selected Poems

WALTER DE LA MARE
Selected Poems

DANIEL DEFOE
A Journal of the Plague Year
Moll Flanders
Robinson Crusoe

CHARLES DICKENS
A Tale of Two Cities
Bleak House
David Copperfield
Dombey and Son
Great Expectations
Hard Times
Little Dorrit
Oliver Twist
The Pickwick Papers

EMILY DICKINSON
Selected Poems

JOHN DONNE
Selected Poems

JOHN DRYDEN
Selected Poems

GERALD DURRELL
My Family and Other Animals

GEORGE ELIOT
Middlemarch
Silas Marner
The Mill on the Floss

T. S. ELIOT
Four Quartets
Murder in the Cathedral
Selected Poems
The Cocktail Party
The Waste Land

J. G. FARRELL
The Siege of Krishnapur

WILLIAM FAULKNER
Absalom, Absalom!
The Sound and the Fury

HENRY FIELDING
Joseph Andrews
Tom Jones

F. SCOTT FITZGERALD
Tender is the Night
The Great Gatsby

GUSTAVE FLAUBERT
Madame Bovary

E. M. FORSTER
A Passage to India
Howards End

JOHN FOWLES
The French Lieutenant's Woman

ATHOL FUGARD
Selected Plays

JOHN GALSWORTHY
Strife

MRS GASKELL
North and South

WILLIAM GOLDING
Lord of the Flies
The Spire

OLIVER GOLDSMITH
She Stoops to Conquer
The Vicar of Wakefield

ROBERT GRAVES
Goodbye to All That

GRAHAM GREENE
Brighton Rock
The Heart of the Matter
The Power and the Glory

WILLIS HALL
The Long and the Short and the Tall

THOMAS HARDY
Far from the Madding Crowd
Jude the Obscure
Selected Poems
Tess of the D'Urbervilles
The Mayor of Casterbridge
The Return of the Native
The Trumpet Major
The Woodlanders
Under the Greenwood Tree

L. P. HARTLEY
The Go-Between
The Shrimp and the Anemone

NATHANIEL HAWTHORNE
The Scarlet Letter

SEAMUS HEANEY
Selected Poems

JOSEPH HELLER
Catch-22

ERNEST HEMINGWAY
A Farewell to Arms
For Whom the Bell Tolls
The Old Man and the Sea

HERMANN HESSE
Steppenwolf

BARRY HINES
Kes

HOMER
The Iliad
The Odyssey

ANTHONY HOPE
The Prisoner of Zenda

GERARD MANLEY HOPKINS
Selected Poems

RICHARD HUGHES
A High Wind in Jamaica

TED HUGHES
Selected Poems

THOMAS HUGHES
Tom Brown's Schooldays

ALDOUS HUXLEY
Brave New World

HENRIK IBSEN
A Doll's House
Ghosts

HENRY JAMES
The Ambassadors
The Portrait of a Lady
Washington Square

SAMUEL JOHNSON
Rasselas

BEN JONSON
The Alchemist
Volpone

JAMES JOYCE
A Portrait of the Artist as a Young Man
Dubliners

JOHN KEATS
Selected Poems

PHILIP LARKIN
Selected Poems

D. H. LAWRENCE
Selected Short Stories
Sons and Lovers
The Rainbow
Women in Love

CAMARA LAYE
L'Enfant Noir

HARPER LEE
To Kill a Mocking-Bird

LAURIE LEE
Cider with Rosie

THOMAS MANN
Tonio Kröger

CHRISTOPHER MARLOWE
Doctor Faustus

ANDREW MARVELL
Selected Poems

W. SOMERSET MAUGHAM
Selected Short Stories

GAVIN MAXWELL
Ring of Bright Water

J. MEADE FALKNER
Moonfleet

HERMAN MELVILLE
Moby Dick

THOMAS MIDDLETON
Women Beware Women

THOMAS MIDDLETON *and* WILLIAM ROWLEY
The Changeling

ARTHUR MILLER
A View from the Bridge
Death of a Salesman
The Crucible

JOHN MILTON
Paradise Lost I & II
Paradise Lost IV & IX
Selected Poems

V. S. NAIPAUL
A House for Mr Biswas

ROBERT O'BRIEN
Z for Zachariah

SEAN O'CASEY
Juno and the Paycock

GABRIEL OKARA
The Voice

EUGENE O'NEILL
Mourning Becomes Electra

GEORGE ORWELL
Animal Farm
Nineteen Eighty-four

JOHN OSBORNE
Look Back in Anger

WILFRED OWEN
Selected Poems

ALAN PATON
Cry, The Beloved Country

THOMAS LOVE PEACOCK
Nightmare Abbey and *Crotchet Castle*

HAROLD PINTER
The Caretaker

SYLVIA PLATH
Selected Works

PLATO
The Republic

ALEXANDER POPE
Selected Poems

J. B. PRIESTLEY
An Inspector Calls
THOMAS PYNCHON
The Crying of Lot 49
SIR WALTER SCOTT
Ivanhoe
Quentin Durward
The Heart of Midlothian
Waverley
PETER SHAFFER
The Royal Hunt of the Sun
WILLIAM SHAKESPEARE
A Midsummer Night's Dream
Antony and Cleopatra
As You Like It
Coriolanus
Cymbeline
Hamlet
Henry IV Part I
Henry IV Part II
Henry V
Julius Caesar
King Lear
Love's Labour's Lost
Macbeth
Measure for Measure
Much Ado About Nothing
Othello
Richard II
Richard III
Romeo and Juliet
Sonnets
The Merchant of Venice
The Taming of the Shrew
The Tempest
The Winter's Tale
Troilus and Cressida
Twelfth Night
GEORGE BERNARD SHAW
Androcles and the Lion
Arms and the Man
Caesar and Cleopatra
Candida
Major Barbara
Pygmalion
Saint Joan
The Devil's Disciple
MARY SHELLEY
Frankenstein
PERCY BYSSHE SHELLEY
Selected Poems
RICHARD BRINSLEY SHERIDAN
The School for Scandal
The Rivals
R. C. SHERRIFF
Journey's End
WOLE SOYINKA
The Road
EDMUND SPENSER
The Faerie Queene (Book I)
JOHN STEINBECK
Of Mice and Men
The Grapes of Wrath
The Pearl

LAURENCE STERNE
A Sentimental Journey
Tristram Shandy
ROBERT LOUIS STEVENSON
Kidnapped
Treasure Island
TOM STOPPARD
Professional Foul
Rosencrantz and Guildenstern are Dead
JONATHAN SWIFT
Gulliver's Travels
JOHN MILLINGTON SYNGE
The Playboy of the Western World
TENNYSON
Selected Poems
W. M. THACKERAY
Vanity Fair
DYLAN THOMAS
Under Milk Wood
FLORA THOMPSON
Lark Rise to Candleford
J. R. R. TOLKIEN
The Hobbit
ANTHONY TROLLOPE
Barchester Towers
MARK TWAIN
Huckleberry Finn
Tom Sawyer
JOHN VANBRUGH
The Relapse
VIRGIL
The Aeneid
VOLTAIRE
Candide
KEITH WATERHOUSE
Billy Liar
EVELYN WAUGH
Decline and Fall
JOHN WEBSTER
The Duchess of Malfi
H. G. WELLS
The History of Mr Polly
The Invisible Man
The War of the Worlds
OSCAR WILDE
The Importance of Being Earnest
THORNTON WILDER
Our Town
TENNESSEE WILLIAMS
The Glass Menagerie
VIRGINIA WOOLF
Mrs Dalloway
To the Lighthouse
WILLIAM WORDSWORTH
Selected Poems
WILLIAM WYCHERLEY
The Country Wife
W. B. YEATS
Selected Poems